"I heard it all," Caroline said angrily.

"The music, the laughing, the groans of passion," she continued.

"Would you please tell me what you're talking about?" Jared demanded.

"Oh, give it up, Jared! You had a woman in the cupola, and it was obvious what was going on. This may be your house, but I have a right not to be subjected to your . . . *carnal escapades.*"

Jared was looking at her as though she'd lost her mind. "Honey, I haven't had any carnal escapades within recent memory. I was at an exceedingly boring meeting last night. Do you have a history of erotic hallucinations?" he teased.

"I'm not a sex-starved spinster with an overactive imagination, thank you very much. I don't have to rely on erotic hallucinations to get my jollies."

Suddenly the scent of lavender wafted through the room, and moonlight gave the room an eerie quality. Caroline shivered. "Maybe it was ghosts," she murmured. "Maybe we stirred up Katherine's and her husband's ghosts."

Dear Reader,

Glenda Sanders has always enjoyed bringing supernatural elements into her romance novels. Readers loved #316 *Dark Secrets* so much that she was inspired to write another spine-tingling romance, *Haunting Secrets*. In *Haunting Secrets*, Glenda has combined her love of ghost lore with her passion for old houses to create a fabulously romantic, deliciously comic and bone-chilling story—a combination so perfect, we just had to make it an Editor's Choice. Let us know the effect it had on you. Please write to us:

The Editors
Harlequin Temptation
225 Duncan Mill Road
Don Mills, Ontario, Canada
M3B 3K9

Haunting Secrets

GLENDA SANDERS

Harlequin Books

TORONTO • NEW YORK • LONDON
AMSTERDAM • PARIS • SYDNEY • HAMBURG
STOCKHOLM • ATHENS • TOKYO • MILAN
MADRID • WARSAW • BUDAPEST • AUCKLAND

Published July 1992

ISBN 0-373-25502-0

HAUNTING SECRETS

1

"COOKIE NAYLOR," Essie Mae Dunmore Berryhill announced.

"Who's that, Aunt Essie?" Jared Colin asked. He was not kin to the imposing matron sitting opposite him—a fact for which he was exceedingly grateful. Still, he used the familiar address that pleased her, not only because it pleased her and cost him nothing, but because he was dependent upon her goodwill.

Essie Mae Dunmore Berryhill viewed the presidency of the Taggartville Historical Preservation Society as a sacred trust, and her latest avocation was acting as watchdog over the renovation of Katherine House, the Victorian monstrosity of a mansion that Jared had inherited from his grandfather. Because Katherine House sat in the heart of the town's historic district and had been officially designated an historic landmark, any structural renovation or exterior decoration fell subject to approval by the society—and *that* approval was dependent upon the goodwill of the society's president.

"Cookie? Why, she's Caroline Naylor's granddaughter, that's who," Essie replied, as though the question had been superfluous. "She was named after Caroline. Her grandpa started calling her Cookie to keep from getting them confused."

"I'm not sure I've met Caroline Naylor," Jared said, reaching into an internal reservoir of patience to keep from shaking Essie Mae Dunmore Berryhill until the hairpins anchoring the blue-rinsed gray bun to the top of her head were dislodged and telling her to get to the point.

Aunt Essie gave a knowing laugh. "Not likely, considering you just moved here this week, and Caroline's been dead nigh on five years."

Jared clamped his teeth together and sucked in a deep breath in an effort to sustain his waning patience with Aunt Essie's convoluted chatter.

A gray eyebrow arched in what he recognized as imperial disapproval. "Well, Caroline's daughter-in-law worked— outside the home, you know—although God only knows why. Caroline's son was some kind of scientist, so they weren't hurting for money. Anyway, Cookie spent her summers here, and she and Caroline were closer than two peas in a pod. Those two used to sew up a storm. Heavens! One summer they made curtains for every room in the youth center!"

"That's fascinating," Jared said, hoping she couldn't hear the growing impatience in his voice. "But I don't see what all this has to do with me."

"Why, Cookie'd be perfect, that's what," Aunt Essie said. "She loves old houses. She and Caroline took a cross-country tour of historic inns just months before Caroline—"

Sighing, she shook her head, and her chin quivered. "She was so young, too."

"Cookie?" Jared asked.

"Caroline!" Aunt Essie corrected. "She was only sixty-eight." Her voice became a confidential whisper. "It was her heart. She went just like—" She snapped age-crooked fingers in the air.

Jared tried to sound appropriately sympathetic. "That's too bad."

"You probably couldn't get her, anyway."

"I beg your pardon?"

"Cookie. She works for some fancy-schmancy decorating firm in Boston. Oh, no, I'm sure she wouldn't be able to . . . But wouldn't it be wonderful if she could?"

She appeared to be waiting for an answer. Jared felt as though he'd been talking over a static-plagued telephone line and hearing every other word. "I suppose," he replied, trying to sound interested but noncommittal, so that Aunt Essie wouldn't know he hadn't the slightest idea what she was talking about.

"I mean, anyone who loves old houses the way Cookie does, and has so much talent, would have to do a marvelous job with Katherine House."

Suddenly all the puzzle pieces of Essie's disjointed conversation fit together. "She certainly sounds like just the person I need," Jared said, quite sincerely. Anyone named Cookie would have to be a natural in a Victorian monstrosity.

"You could check," Aunt Essie suggested hopefully.

"Didn't you say she works in Boston?"

Essie Mae Dunmore Berryhill's spine stiffened. "Her *mother* was from New England. An old family, I understand. Real Boston Brahmins. Relatives probably came over on the *Mayflower*. She met Caroline's son when he was studying at MIT, and talked him into staying up north. But Cookie's a lovely girl."

Jared grinned at the last, tacked-on assurance. *Despite her mother's Yankee influence* was implied in the statement. Essie Mae Dunmore Berryhill took being a Southerner, specifically a Floridian, as seriously as she took the preservation of local history.

"I'm sure she is, but—"

"I get a Christmas card from Cookie every year—she's such a thoughtful girl. I'm sure I have the name of the firm she works for."

"I guess I *could* give her a call," Jared said. If she happened to be available, he'd have the decorator he needed; if not, he'd at least have made the effort, which should earn him some goodwill points with Aunt Essie.

Aunt Essie clutched the handle of the large purse in her lap and heaved herself out of the chair. "I really have to go," she said. "It's the second Wednesday. Bridge day at the community center, you know."

Jared hadn't known, but he nodded, then rose and offered his elbow to Aunt Essie so he could escort her from his office through the maze of ladders and drop cloths cluttering the Grand Salon of the mansion. Essie paused in the doorway and gave the workmen stripping the wainscoting a sharp-eyed inspection, then turned back to Jared. "There's good work being done here. It's refreshing to see someone truly dedicated to the preservation of history."

"Katherine House was very special to my grandfather. I'm sure he would have wanted me to do everything I can to preserve it."

A withered hand landed on Jared's forearm. "You're a good boy, Jared. The governor would be proud of you."

SLEET FELL FROM DISMAL gray skies, adding to the layer of ice and muddied snow that lined the curbs. Caroline Naylor looked past Danitra's moussed-and-scrunched hair to watch the freezing drizzle through the window. Three o'clock, and it was already dark and bleak; at five o'clock it would be even darker and bleaker. Her car would be colder than a coffin, and it would take her apartment half an hour to progress from frigid to bearable, once she got home and turned up the heat. The very thought sent a shiver up Caroline's spine. Winter had never been her favorite time of year, and this particular winter had been nastier than most.

Danitra, oblivious to weather and other mortal concerns, was conducting the weekly staff meeting with her usual aplomb. Grinning slyly, she opened a portfolio and skimmed over it during what could only be classified as a dramatic pause. "I saved the best for last: the Claxton Corporation.

We're still awaiting final word, but they were *wild* about our preliminary sketches."

She practically sang the last sentence. Caroline noted with exasperation that Danitra had used the regal *our*. Sketches were always the sole property of the individual designer until a client loved them. Then they became the property of the Urbane! Interiors, and since Danitra *was* Urbane! Interiors, they became her ideas too—just as the credit became hers.

Caroline crossed her right leg over her left in an effort to prevent fidgeting in the ultramodern purple-and-puce chair that faced Danitra's desk. Danitra's penchant for high drama had lost its luster after the second or third performance. Caroline now calculated that since this was her fourth year in Danitra's employ, she'd endured Danitra's weekly performances somewhere in the neighborhood of two hundred times.

Not for the first time, or the hundredth, she wondered if it wasn't time to make a change. She'd learned as much as she was going to learn from Danitra, gained enough experience to look impressive on a résumé, and made contacts throughout the industry. And she hadn't had a vacation in two years.

Staring out the window, Caroline watched the sleet fall in the early twilight. She'd lost track of Danitra's closing remarks and realized she didn't care. She sighed softly. Yes, it was definitely time for a change—or a vacation.

An hour later she was at her own desk when the receptionist, Dolores, buzzed her. "I may get fired for asking this, but do you answer to the name Cookie?"

"Not since—" Caroline's voice faltered. Not since her grandmother's death. The only people who'd called her Cookie were the people in Taggartville. "Not for a long time. Why?"

"There's a Mr. Colin on line two who asked for Miss Cookie Naylor," Dolores said. "He was very insistent about talking to you."

Caroline searched through a cobwebbed part of her brain for any Mr. Colin her grandmother might have known. The only thing that came to mind was the Colin's bread her grandmother always bought. "A Mr. Colin, you say?"

"That's right. Colin."

"I'll take it," Caroline said, her curiosity piqued. "Oh...Dolores?"

"Yes, *Cookie*," Dolores answered, in what Caroline surmised was destined to be the first of many teasing taunts to come.

"Does he sound—" She sought an appropriate word. "Elderly?"

Dolores's chortled "Ha!" reverberated through the line. "*Au contraire*, Cookie. He sounds like a hunk and a half."

"Curiouser and curiouser," Caroline muttered, then thanked Dolores before punching the line-two button. Her tone grew crisply professional. "Caroline Naylor."

"Ms. Naylor. My name is Jared Colin. You don't know me, but Essie Mae Dunmore Berryhill—"

"Aunt Essie!" Caroline exclaimed, envisioning the blue-rinsed whirling dervish of a woman. "I haven't seen Aunt Essie since my grandmother's funeral."

On the other end of the line, Jared cleared his throat, hunting for the proper response to Caroline's exuberance. The warmth that had crept into Cookie Naylor's throaty voice had given it a sensuous quality that surprised him. He'd assumed that Cookie Naylor, granddaughter of the late Caroline Naylor, would resemble Aunt Essie's granddaughters, both of whom were active in the Taggartville Historical Preservation Society—both sturdy, middle-aged, staid, salt-of-the-earth types. This voice sounded as though its owner might be wearing satin underwear.

Lace, he corrected mentally. *Sexy, peek-a-boo, tease-a-man-to-the-brink-of-insanity midnight-blue lace.*

Realizing that The Voice was now silent, and that it was customary, in social conversations, for the person who'd last been spoken to to speak, he cleared his throat and grasped for something he hoped sounded coherent. "I own a house."

"Oh?"

Jared thought into the dead silence that followed that Cookie of The Voice probably thought she was talking to a half-wit. Or a pervert. Jared frowned at the possibility that she might be right, at least temporarily. This Katherine House project, which had seemed so simple in the idea stage, had proven to be quite vexing in practice, but he hadn't realized how far off-center he'd veered until this very moment. Who would have thought that the sound of the voice of a woman he'd never met could send him foraying into vivid sexual fantasy? The paint-remover fumes must be making him light-headed.

He needed to get away from the construction confusion in Katherine House. He needed a reprieve from Essie Mae Dunmore Berryhill and the Taggartville Historical Preservation Society.

He needed . . . a woman.

"You may be familiar with my house," he said, hoping to salvage the task at hand, which, he reminded himself, was hiring a decorator to restore his house. "It's a Victorian mon—mansion. They call it Katherine House."

"Katherine House?" The Voice said, growing even warmer. "You mean Old Man Taggart's house?"

"That's the one."

Caroline remembered that the old mansion, home to an aging recluse, had been the inspiration for much speculation about ghouls and ghosts and assorted less supernatural, creepy, crawly things when she'd been in elementary school. "We used to call it Crackpot House."

"Crackpot House?"

"Because of the eccentric old man who lived there. Rumor had it he was over a hundred years old."

"A hundred and three when he finally kicked the bucket."

"Is it haunted, too?"

"Is it supposed to be?"

"What venerable old Victorian mansion with a resident eccentric isn't?"

"Well, if it is, that should be good for business."

"Business?"

"I'm converting it to a tearoom and inn."

"I see," The Voice ventured noncommittally.

"I've been working with the Taggartville Historical Preservation Society through Aunt Essie."

"Oh." The word was impregnated with sudden understanding.

"You're familiar with the society, then?" Jared asked.

"Mmm." The Voice slithered through the line like a velvet-skinned snake to wrap itself around his senses, leading Jared to the conclusion that he *definitely* needed a woman soon.

"The downstairs is almost done," he said. "But I need help with the upper stories. Aunt Essie thought you might be uniquely qualified to supervise the renovation, particularly of Katherine's personal rooms."

"Is it true that Old Man Taggart never went upstairs and wouldn't let anyone up there except to clean, and insisted that everything be left exactly the way it was when his wife died?" The voice was animated by fascination—and Jared was even more fascinated by The Voice.

"What we found up there certainly lends credence to the legend," Jared said. "It was bizarre. We've done some preliminary cleaning—the house was empty for a year, and a family of squirrels got into a lot of mischief—but we were careful to photograph every detail before we touched anything, and kept samples of all the fabrics and wall coverings. What we need now is someone to put it all back together."

Caroline hoped he couldn't hear her drooling over the prospect of working on Katherine House. She'd only been fascinated by it since she was knee-high to a grasshopper.

Jared wasn't sure what to read into the silence on the other end of the line. "It would require at least six weeks, maybe longer. I don't know what your arrangement is with Urbane!, but we could contract you through them, or you could take a leave of absence and contract as an independent."

Or I could use the vacation time I've accrued and take a working vacation doing a dream assignment, Caroline thought.

"Please consider it," Jared said.

He heard what could have been either an indrawn breath or a sigh before The Voice, sounding efficient, said, "Let me get this straight. You want me to delegate the project I'm working on at Urbane! so that I can spend endless hours looking at fabric samples and special wallpaper books and prowl through dozens of antique shops in order to restore the rooms in your house."

"That about sums it up," Jared replied. "Oh, and I'd like to get started right away if you decide to take it on."

Caroline cast a baleful glance at the freezing rain falling outside her window. "You want me to abandon Massachusetts during the most severe winter in the past century and drive to Florida, where it's probably sunny and mild and the snowbirds and tourists are running around in Bermuda shorts and halter tops?"

The inflection in The Voice managed to make it sound as though he were a devil bartering for her soul. "Well—"

"You just hired yourself a decorator!"

"Just like that?"

"Did you want a résumé and portfolio?" The Voice challenged.

"No. I mean, yes. For the files. A formality. It's just . . . Don't you want to quibble over rates?"

Rates! Caroline thought. In her ecstasy over the prospect of escaping the frozen hinterlands, she'd forgotten she'd be making money for doing what she'd always wanted to do in her most extravagant Walter Mitty dreams. "I assume you know what the going rate for a quality decorator is," she said.

"Yes, but—"

"You wouldn't try to cheat me, would you?"

Before Jared could assure her he was a man of principle, The Voice threatened, "I'd just have to sic Aunt Essie on you if you did."

"Heaven forbid!" Jared said. The prospect was enough to make a mafia *patrono* wary.

Convinced that he sounded suitably intimidated, Caroline decided to push for some perks. "I'd need a place to stay."

If Cookie Naylor looked as good as she sounded, Jared knew one parlor she was welcome in. Reminding himself that a disembodied voice was seldom a reflection of its owner's physical manifestation, he tried to sound like a serious business negotiator. "As long as you don't expect a suite at the Ritz."

"I don't recall a Ritz or any similar accommodation in Taggartville," Caroline said. "I live simply. A furnished room somewhere would suffice, preferably with a private bath."

"That should be easily arranged. I'll confer with Aunt Essie. If there's a room to be had, she'll find it."

"And mileage," The Voice pressed sweetly.

"Take the interstate," Jared advised.

"I'll be there—" Caroline paused to calculate how long it would take her to dig out her summer wardrobe and drive a good portion of the Eastern seaboard. "—On Wednesday."

"I look forward to working with you," Jared said. *To seeing you.* Ah, the bodies and faces his mind would assign The

Voice over the next five days! He hung up the phone feeling smug with accomplishment.

Scarcely three minutes passed before his phone rang. "Jared Colin," he growled into the receiver, irritated at having a particularly vivid fantasy rudely interrupted.

"I forgot about Desdemona," The Voice informed him.

"What's a Desdemona?" Jared asked. Exotic diseases came to mind. A noisome skin rash, perhaps.

"Desdemona is a cat," The Voice explained. "My cat. She's such a baby! I couldn't possibly leave her for an entire month, even if I knew someone who'd take her for that length of time. And a kennel is out of the question. So she's coming with me."

Jared didn't know how he was supposed to respond to the challenge that had crept into The Voice, so he said nothing.

"I thought you'd want to know."

"That you're bringing a cat?"

"Because of the room," The Voice explained with the slightest edge of impatience at having been compelled to explain something so obvious. "Some landlords don't allow pets, so I thought you'd want—need—to know about Desdemona."

"Oh."

"I didn't want you to get stuck in an irrevocable lease with some boardinghouse that doesn't take pets."

The idea of an irrevocable lease with a boardinghouse in Taggartville was laughable, but Jared reminded himself that Cookie, custodian of The Voice, was from A Big City Up North. "I see," he said. "Well, thanks for letting me know."

There was an awkward moment of silence before The Voice responded, "Until Wednesday, then?"

"Yes," Jared agreed. "Until Wednesday." He hung up, with disappointment settling heavily on his shoulders.

Ye gods! A cat named Desdemona. Images of midnight-blue lace and come-hither smiles dissolved in a poof, to be replaced by images of a pampered white Persian rubbing against support-hose-encased thick ankles protruding from sensible thick-soled shoes, and a stubby-fingered hand reaching down to administer loving strokes while The Voice crooned, in baby talk, "You're *such* a baby, aren't you?"

Let it never be said that Jared Colin had a problem with reality!

2

SHORTLY AFTER NOON ON Wednesday, Caroline parked in front of the Victorian mansion that had inspired many a spooky tale and romantic daydream when she was growing up. The venerable old house was eerily unchanged, except for a bronze marker on the front lawn.

Katherine House

Built at the turn of the century by railroad magnate Augustus Taggart, this landmark winter cottage renowned for its distinctive "kaleidoscope" cupola with stained-glass windows was first occupied year-round by Taggart's son, Samuel Augustus Taggart. It is named for Samuel Taggart's wife, Katherine Colin Taggart, who occupied the house with her husband from their marriage in 1919 until her death in 1930. Mr. Taggart remained in the house until his death in 1973 at the age of 103. Ownership of the house then passed to Katherine Taggart's brother, Florida Governor Mitchell Colin, who willed it to his grandson, Jared Colin.

Katherine House is on the National Register of Historic Places.

Caroline craned her neck to look at the intricate stained-glass mosaics set into the sloping roof of the cupola. She'd been fascinated by the colorful glass motifs as a child, especially after her grandmother had told her that sunlight shin-

ing through the mosaics cast a constantly changing kalei-
doscopelike pattern on the rosewood floor of the third-story
cupola room. Many times she'd sat in the oak tree in her
grandmother's front yard and tried to imagine what that
room must be like, with spots of color dancing on the floor;
but no one had been allowed inside Katherine House except
the housekeeper and handyman who worked for Old Man
Taggart, and the nurse who sometimes pushed the wizened
old man's wheelchair onto the wraparound veranda so he
could bask in the shade on lazy summer afternoons.

Caroline and her Taggartville playmates had seen him
there, shriveled and waxy-skinned, staring vacantly into
space while his nurse sat nearby in a metal glider, crocheting
and humming "Amazing Grace."

"We're looking at history," Caroline had whispered to Billy
Shelton.

"That's dumb," Billy had replied. "It's just Old Man Taggart."

"My grandma says he's part of history," Caroline insisted.
"He's over a hundred years old."

"People cain't be history, and even if they could, it wouldn't
be some old man who's pair-of-lized."

"What's pair-of-lized?"

"He cain't move. My mom said he got some kind of stroke.
And even if he could move, he's crazy."

"He's very old," Caroline had conceded, "but that doesn't
make him crazy."

Billy had given her a look of pure male intolerance. "Ev-
erybody knows Old Man Taggart is loony as a Bessie bug. His
wife got killed on a train, and he never went upstairs again,
and never let nobody else upstairs in that collidascope room,
neither."

Caroline had sighed. "If I had a room where light danced
on the floor, I'd sit up there and watch it all day long."

"*She* used to sit up there," Billy had told her. "That's why Old Man Taggart wouldn't go up there no more, 'cause he was 'fraid he'd see her ghost or something."

"There's no such things as ghosts," Caroline had said. Even as she had denied the possibility, though, she'd felt a thrill at the prospect of Katherine Taggart's ghost haunting the Kaleidoscope Room, and wondered if the color-tinted sunlight would pass straight through a ghost on its way to dance on the rosewood floor.

Caroline sighed again at the memory of that long-ago summer day. She now viewed the stained glass with an adult's appreciation of the craftsmanship required to execute such intricate work. Lowering her head, she absently massaged her neck to prevent a crick and followed the walk to the house. As Caroline stepped onto the wraparound veranda, a floorboard groaned like a living creature being disturbed from deep sleep.

Desdemona, apparently nervous over the change from routine, answered the creak of the wood with a bloodcurdling howl that raised goose pimples on Caroline's scalp. Caroline immediately put the cat carrier down and knelt beside it, uttering assurances to the feline. "It's all right, Dessie. Take it easy, girl. It was just old wood."

Once the cat was quiet, Caroline said, "You can stay here a moment. I'm going to see if anyone's home. We don't have to bother with doorbells, do we? That cry of yours was enough to wake the dead."

The door was locked tight and no one answered, even after Caroline banged the ornate bronze knocker.

Caroline debated what to do. She could hardly fault Mr. Colin for not being there to welcome her now when she wasn't expected until midafternoon. Still, she was restless after the long drive, hungry, and in need of a ladies' room; certainly she was in neither a mood nor a condition to sit down on the porch steps and wait—possibly for hours—for her new boss to show up. So she picked up Desdemona's carrier and headed back to her car, careful to avoid the creaking floorboard as she crossed the veranda.

Although she'd passed some fast-food places on her way into town, in her mind there was only one real place to eat lunch in Taggartville. She drove up Oak Street and turned onto Main, hoping to discover that the Cow Café had survived the blight of creeping urbanization.

Technically, it was Mrs. O'Leary's Cow Café, but the Mrs. O'Leary's had always been written in small print above the two shorter words. To the natives it always had been, and always would be, the Cow Café—gathering place of local politicos and community leaders, and clearinghouse for world news and local gossip.

The Cow Café cuisine was simple, stick-to-the-ribs fare either personally prepared by Mrs. O'Leary or prepared under her watchful eye. *Mrs. O'Leary,* Caroline thought. Could she possibly still be around? She'd seemed so old. Although, thinking back, Caroline realized that Mrs. O'Leary couldn't have been all that old; her youngest son, Marty, was just a few years older than Caroline.

The Cow Café was, indeed, still open. Although the sign was new and larger than ever, the café itself, housed between two shops in a long row, was unchanged. Caroline parallel-parked along the curb.

From inside the café, Jared observed the arrival of the sporty compact with idle interest, assuming that some sightseer must have ventured off the normal tourist trails. He hadn't seen this car around town, and the retirees who wintered in Florida generally preferred conservative luxury models.

He sat up a bit straighter in the hard wooden chair when the door on the driver's side opened and a curtain of blond hair emerged into his field of vision, followed by feminine shoulders covered by peach linen. As the driver turned, shoving the door closed, Jared caught sight of her face, and his breath lodged in his throat. *Hell-o mama! Wanna play house?* He'd been so buried in work since moving to Taggartville that he'd forgotten that women that good-looking existed. Well, not forgotten; he'd merely suppressed the memory to keep from going crazy. But there she was—sleek, beautiful, her fair hair glimmering in the midday sun. Who was she? And what was she doing in Taggartville?

He continued watching as she walked around the car, deciding that she must be a sales representative for some large company. Her city shorts and jacket were appropriate for the climate, but too high-fashion for Florida, land of polyester pantsuits, Bermuda shorts and tourist T's. She opened the passenger door and leaned inside to take something from the backseat—a sample case, perhaps—but Jared quit anything as logical as speculation when her shorts strained across well-shaped buttocks.

He was still staring as she backed out, extracting a large plastic case, and continued staring as she lifted it level with her face and talked to it.

Talked to it? He did a double take! It wasn't a sample case at all, but a pet carrier—the kind used to transport cats or dogs.

Cats? She had a cat? As quickly as the idea came to him, he discounted the possibility. He wasn't even sure there was a cat in that carrier, and even if there was, lots of people traveled with cats—especially women. Just because she was a stranger with Big City written all over her didn't mean this was the spinster decorator Aunt Essie had referred him to. And yet . . . How many strangers showed up at the Cow Café carrying a cat? He would have traded one of his smaller companies for a glimpse of the license plate on the back of that snappy little car.

She lowered the carrying case, holding it suitcase-style by the handle, and looked up, directly into the front window of the café. Catching him staring, she stiffened slightly, her wariness evident. Reflexively, he smiled, hoping to put her at ease. Apparently it worked, because she relaxed noticeably and, with a slight shrug of her shoulders, returned a self-conscious smile before starting into the café.

You're not in the big city now, she was thinking. *People in small towns stare at strangers. Besides, he doesn't look like a pervert or a mass murderer.* The man in the window, in fact, looked like anything but a pervert or a mass killer. He was nicely dressed and impeccably groomed and almost scandalously handsome.

So was that charming serial killer, Ted Bundy, an inner voice reminded.

Quit being such a ninny! she argued back. *This is Taggartville and the Cow Café. Ask one question about him and you'll know his name, social security number, astrological birth sign and what childhood diseases he had by the time you leave.*

Her first sensation, as she entered the café, was one of déjà vu. How could it be so unchanged, as though time had stood still? There were the same linoleum floor, wooden tables and checkered tablecloths; the same glass-fronted cashier's stand with its racks of candy bars and chewing gum. The old blackboard, with a humorous cartoon cow and the heading, How Now, Mrs. O'Leary's Cow? still hung above the pass-through window between the dining room and kitchen, quietly announcing the daily special. The place even smelled the same! The air was redolent with the scent of simmering food and warming bread, of bacon from breakfast and cinnamon from freshly baked rolls and apple pie.

The dining room, which probably had been filled to capacity at the peak of the lunch hour, was clearing out. Caroline felt the curious scrutiny of the diners who remained, and was careful to avoid looking in the direction of the windows, where her dark, mysterious admirer was seated.

Marty O'Leary, twice as many pounds heavier as he was years older than the last time Caroline had seen him, was manning the cash register. He gave Caroline a cursory nod of welcome, then, with recognition obviously dawning at second glance, chuckled. "I'll be damned. Cookie Naylor?"

Caroline had unabashedly flirted with Marty O'Leary the summer she was fifteen. By the time she returned the next year, he was engaged to marry the head cheerleader from a rival high school in a neighboring town. After a year of fantasizing about her long-distance love, Caroline had been devastated—until two days later, when she'd discovered the lifeguard at the YMCA pool, a college man with a broad chest and a thick thatch of blond hair.

Caroline returned Marty's warm laugh and stepped up to the counter to offer him her right hand for shaking. "Most people call me Caroline, nowadays. Hello, Marty."

"I heard you were coming to town."

"Oh?" Caroline replied. For a moment she was surprised that he'd heard about her return, and then she remembered Taggartville's gossip grapevine and Aunt Essie. Aunt Essie would never be accused of hoarding titillating morsels of information, and sooner or later, every snippet of interesting news wound up as fodder for discussion at the Cow Café.

"You here for lunch?"

"You bet. But I have a bit of a problem." She pointed at the plastic pet carrier on the floor near her feet.

"That a cat?" Marty asked incredulously.

"I know that it's not strictly legal to bring her into a restaurant, but I couldn't leave her in the car."

Marty laughed. "This is no restaurant. It's the Cow Café. As long as she stays in the box, shouldn't be any problem."

"Thanks," Caroline said, reaching down for the carrier.

Jared distinctly heard Marty O'Leary call the woman Cookie. Realizing his advantage at being able to observe her without her knowledge, he shifted his gaze from the pet carrier to a pair of decidedly *unthick* ankles above flat-but-stylish shoes, then lifted it to long, shapely calves and cute-as-a-button knees. He reconnoitered sleek thighs until his eyes encountered the hemline of a pair of tailored shorts. Frustrated by that dead end, he raised his gaze to the tasteful but oh-so-enticing hint of cleavage at the vee of her shirt; to a long, graceful neck and delicately rounded jaw; and, finally, to a classic oval face framed by shoulder-length hair.

Some Cookie! Class. Breeding. Yankee sophistication. Girl-next-door wholesomeness. Jared felt more than a bit hot under the collar. The last time he'd had a stroke of luck this good had been in business—and he'd cleared almost a million bucks in bottom-line profit.

"Special's meat loaf today," Marty told Caroline.

"Sounds delicious."

"You find yourself a seat and I'll put in the order. When Momma finds out you're here, she'll probably bring it out personally."

Still careful to avoid looking in the direction of the window, Caroline scanned the center and back of the room. She'd targeted a small table along the wall and was weaving her way toward it when her intended path was suddenly cut off by the man from the window.

He was even better-looking up close than he had appeared from a distance. Wearing white pleated pants and a navy-and-white awning-stripe shirt, he seemed almost to shine. But as outrageous as his clothes were, they suited him, providing a counterpoint to his classic handsomeness and underscoring the sense of fun hinted at by his affable grin.

Charisma. The word popped into Caroline's mind in the split second before he spoke to her, in that fleeting moment when they both seemed frozen in place, but during which her mind was wildly active, preparing her to parry the inevitable come-on.

Joe Charisma bent over, peering into the window of the cat carrier. "Desdemona, I presume?"

Caroline was granting him points for originality of approach when it occurred to her that she hadn't mentioned the cat's name since coming into the café. The only person she'd told the name to was—

Sure, Aunt Essie had consistently referred to him as a nice young man. But Aunt Essie was prone to referring to anyone on the minus side of half a century as "nice young man" or "such a sweet girl." Caroline had assumed that any man who'd started out rich and accumulated a fortune in his own right would be closer to the half-century mark than the quarter-century mark. This man was on the shy side of thirty. "Jared Colin?" she sputtered.

The affable grin reappeared as he offered his right hand. "If that's Desdemona, you must be my decorator. Welcome to Taggartville, Cookie."

3

HER EXPRESSION WAS SO peculiar that for a few seconds Jared suffered a sinking feeling in his gut that he'd leaped to all the wrong conclusions. "You are Cookie Naylor, aren't you?"

"Yes," she said, with a slight shake of her head. Then, with a smile, she added, "I'm sorry. It's just that it's been a while since anyone called me that. Maybe we should go with Caroline."

"Caroline it is, then," he said, and with his most charming smile, inquired, "May I carry your cat?"

"She's not—" Caroline began but he was already reaching for the carrier. "—Heavy," she completed futilely as his fingers deftly wove through hers to wrap around the handle and relieve her of the burden.

"Over here," he said, leading her to the window-side table where he'd been seated earlier.

Caroline looked at the tabletop, taking in the two empty plates, the sweating glasses of water and iced tea near each plate. "You've already eaten," she said, wondering who had originally shared the table with him and noting with an unjustifiable stab of irritation that there were lipstick smears on the glass at the side of the table at which he was pulling out a chair for her.

"I'll have dessert," he said smoothly, and sat down opposite her. Immediately a waitress in jeans, T-shirt and apron scurried over to clear away the used dishes and put a fresh paper place-mat and flatware in front of Caroline.

"Can I get you something to drink?"

"Iced tea," Caroline said curtly, remembering the lipstick smear on the glass that had just been lifted off the table.

"I could bring a bowl of water for the kitty," the waitress offered.

Caroline looked at her, really noticing her face for the first time. She was young, pretty in a natural, wholesome way, and sincere. Caroline smiled. "There's a lick bottle inside the carrier, but thank you for offering."

"Mrs. O'Leary will be out with your meat loaf in a minute," the girl said, and then scurried away.

"I'd forgotten," Caroline remarked.

Jared caught her meaning. "It's a different world, isn't it?"

"It's nice. I was ready for a change of pace."

"When you get desperate for a touch of life in the big city, Orlando's just half an hour up the road," Jared said wryly.

Head tilted at an inquisitive angle, Caroline speculated, "You prefer city living?"

"I like the best of both worlds."

"Very diplomatic," Caroline said. *A politician's answer.*

He had a politician's smile, too: a broad, friendly smile perfect enough to sell toothpaste—or just about anything else aimed at a target market of women. Caroline was not immune to the effect of his stunning good looks. Jet-black hair tumbled over his forehead and tickled his collar. His cheeks were smoothly shaven, but his beard was so dark it gave the illusion of a five-o'clock shadow—a blatantly male, rugged touch on a face characterized by perfect bone structure. And, as though high cheekbones, well-formed lips, a slender nose and strong jaw weren't a potent enough combination, there were his eyes—shockingly blue, vibrant, expressive; bedroom eyes in a movie-star face.

Caroline was glad when Mrs. O'Leary arrived with meat loaf, mashed potatoes, green beans, and a basket of warm rolls. All of these she served to Caroline along with effusive greetings and exclamations over how great Caroline looked, calling her Cookie throughout, while Jared looked on with an expression of benign amusement.

When the furor subsided, Mrs. O'Leary greeted Jared. "Mr. Colin, I didn't know you were here."

"He's already had lunch," said the waitress, who'd arrived with Caroline's iced tea, in a tone that held a subtle hint of disapproval. Caroline surmised that she, too, remembered the glass with the lipstick smears and thought it a bit peculiar that Jared Colin was buying women lunch in shifts. *Take a number, stand in line . . . Next, please!*

Oblivious to—or simply ignoring—the waitress's subtle censure, Jared greeted Mrs. O'Leary by name, gifting her with an easy, lady-killer smile that brought a coquettish glow to her cheeks and a motherly gleam into her eyes. "I understand Cookie's going to be working for you at Katherine House."

"That's right," Jared replied, winking broadly at Caroline. That man was too charming for his own good. Or hers! "She came highly recommended."

A hollow silence followed. "Aunt Essie," Caroline explained, finally.

"Aunt Essie. Of course," Mrs. O'Leary said, and pinned Jared with a sharp look. "I'm just glad you're going to keep Katherine House intact instead of tearing her down. Too many old landmarks are being destroyed these days. 'Course, you open that tearoom for lunch, and we're going to be competitors."

"You know perfectly well no one's going to steal your business, Mrs. O'Leary. You've got the city-hall crowd sewn up."

"The Cow does all right," Mrs. O'Leary admitted, plainly pleased by his deference. "Well, you two probably have a lot to talk about, and I've got to get back to the kitchen. What kind of pie you want?"

"You got any of that great apple cobbler?" Jared asked.

"Sure do. You like it warm, with ice cream, right?"

"Mrs. O'Leary, you keep sweet-talking me like that, and I'm going to have to marry you!"

He was smiling again. He was a charmer, Caroline thought. *And he knew it.*

Rolling her eyes at his outrageousness, Mrs. O'Leary turned to Caroline. "You want the same?"

Caroline hesitated, and Jared coaxed, "You won't believe Mrs. O'Leary's apple cobbler. It melts on your palate."

"I grew up on Mrs. O'Leary's apple cobbler," Caroline said sweetly, then smiled at Mrs. O'Leary. "How could I resist?"

Mrs. O'Leary nodded and walked off toward the kitchen. The idea of eating under the scrutiny of her new employer held little appeal for Caroline, but she was hungry, and the aroma wafting up from the meat loaf was irresistible. Resolutely she picked up her fork and tried not to dwell on the knowledge that the handsomest man south of the Mason-Dixon Line was surreptitiously observing her over the rim of his coffee cup.

The waitress was at the table with dessert within seconds after Caroline put her fork down. Jared attacked his cobbler with the enthusiasm of a man who hadn't had a square meal in at least a week. Caroline took a small spoonful and relished every calorie as it rested on her tongue and then slid down her throat—on its way to her hips, if she didn't watch what she ate over the next few days.

"I stopped at Katherine House on the way into town," she said, after taking a sip of coffee.

His eyes took on warmth, a hint of sensuality as he looked at her directly. "I'm sorry I wasn't there."

Caroline suddenly developed a strong interest in watching the ice cream melt into her cobbler. "I'm anxious to see the house." Abruptly, she raised her gaze to his. "I feel as though I've been waiting to see the inside of Katherine House all my life."

Well, his life had certainly taken an abrupt turn for the better with the arrival of Miss Cookie Naylor, Jared thought. He'd been in Taggartville for nearly four months and he'd had exactly one date, and that had been with an old college girl-friend who'd been passing through the area.

But it wasn't just his temporary deprivation that made the woman seated across from him appealing. She was his type, and on the high end of the scale of what he liked in a woman. Her classy looks, her confident attitude. Those legs! And that voice! The Boston inflection tempered by a trace of down-home, Southern, girl-next-door drawl that hinted of passions bubbling beneath the surface of her cool veneer. She was some package, all right, this Cookie Naylor. And she'd been delivered straight to his door by none other than Taggartville's leading citizen: Aunt Essie.

He thought wryly that this must have been how the wolf felt when Little Red Riding Hood showed up on Grandma's doorstep with a basket of goodies. "I'll give you the dollar tour," he promised, then grinned engagingly and winked. "Most people just get the two-bit walk-through."

Twenty minutes later Caroline once again carried Desde-mona up the walk to Katherine House. Jared had arrived ahead of her and was unlocking the door. After entering the house, he propped the door open with a telephone book. "Sorry about the smell. The chemicals the workers use get a little strong when the house is closed up."

Caroline was too awed by the grandeur of Katherine House to notice the acrid scent of paint remover and sealants. The door, located center front, opened into a Grand Salon with high ceilings, natural wood floors, gingerbread-trimmed archways, and intricate wainscoting. With her decorator's eye, Caroline saw past the ladders, plastic drop cloths and assorted rags, brushes and protective face masks scattered about. Selecting an out-of-the-way spot for Desdemona's carrier, she put it down, then slowly walked the circumference of the room, looking at it from every corner, absorbing and appreciating the proportions of the room and the genius of its design.

"The walls are prepped for new wallpaper as soon as you choose a pattern," Jared said. "This'll be the main dining area for the tearoom, of course. The original dining room of the house is through that door."

There were three doors along one side wall, another on the back wall, and a balustraded stairway on the other side. He indicated the door on the back wall, then followed as Caroline entered a rectangular room that ran the width of the Grand Salon itself. "I thought we'd leave this like it is to accommodate large groups and luncheon meetings."

"May I?" Caroline asked, lifting the corner of the drop cloth protecting the table and chairs. She gasped at the beauty of the mahogany dining set hidden beneath the muslin covering, and instinctively reached out to trace the lines of the carving on the table's apron. "This set is in phenomenal condition."

"It's part of the original furnishings," Jared said. "I don't know how much you know about the history of the house, but since it's remained in a single family, it's never been dismantled, so to speak, like so many others, or allowed to fall into ill repair. And for all that, the furniture has had little wear relative to its age."

"Is there any truth to the legend that Old Man Taggart moved downstairs after his wife died because he couldn't bear to live with her memories on the upper floors?"

"It's true that he moved downstairs," Jared said. "Although there's some speculation that his arthritis had as much to do with his great romantic gesture as his painful memories. Once you climb those stairs, you'll understand why the upper floors held little appeal for an aging man with bad joints."

"How unromantic."

"Ah!" Jared exclaimed, with a mischievous twinkle in his eye as he gave her one of his lady-killer smiles. "So Cookie Naylor is a romantic at heart."

"Caroline. And if you mean that I prefer inconsolable grief to arthritis, I guess that makes me a romantic."

He laughed. "A cautious one. Come on, let's see the kitchen. Then I'll show you the rooms Taggart moved into."

The kitchen was to the left. "This used to be just a pantry," he said. "Originally, food was brought in from the hotel across the street, like at most of the winter cottages. When Taggart moved in year-round, he had a small outkitchen built. My great-aunt moved the kitchen inside in the mid-twenties, taking in the back parlor on this side."

"Your great-aunt?"

"Katherine Taggart was my grandfather's sister."

"Of course. I just hadn't put two and two together." She gave him a small smile. "It must be interesting being related to a legend. I understand she was very beautiful."

"Beautiful enough at sixteen to prompt a forty-nine-year-old confirmed bachelor into proposing, almost at first sight. Have you heard the story?"

"Something about her going door-to-door selling bread?"

"My great-grandfather was killed in World War I. He was quite a hero. Won a boxful of medals. But his death left my great-grandmother widowed with two kids to raise. She was a great cook, so she baked bread and sent my Great-Aunt Katherine and my grandfather out to sell the loaves door-to-door. They always came to the back door of the mansion, of course, and dealt with the housekeeper, but one day Taggart answered the door. The story goes that after seeing Katherine just once, he dressed up in his finest suit and marched up to my great-grandmother's house and asked for her hand in marriage."

"A grand passion," Caroline said.

"You *are* a romantic!" Jared teased.

"He was moved to propose to her after one meeting. That's terribly romantic. Especially when it must have seemed so inappropriate at the time, given their ages and the difference in their social positions in the community."

"He was a horny old man. Maybe he was approaching his fiftieth birthday and didn't want to be alone anymore."

"But he proposed, and she married him."

"An old man's folly and a young girl's romantic whim!"

It was Caroline's turn to tease Jared, and she allowed her gaze to meet his as she said, "Cynic! Don't you believe in love at first sight?"

"It was raging hormones at best. She couldn't possibly have loved him, but she might have been awed by this mansion and the romance of the moment. She was smart enough to see that he could get her family out of their hand-to-mouth existence. Which he did, by the way. He built my great-grandmother a bakery, which grew into Colin's Breads."

"My grandmother always bought Mrs. Colin's bread," Caroline said.

"*Everyone* in the area buys Colin's bakery products. It's the largest commercial bakery in Florida. Anyway, Taggart sent my grandfather to college. Katherine was en route to Tallahassee for his graduation ceremonies when she was killed."

"The Tragic Derailment of 1930," Caroline said.

Jared nodded. "My grandfather always felt responsible. If not for him, she wouldn't have been on that train."

"How could anyone have known that that embankment was going to wash out?" Caroline asked.

"Intellectually he knew he wasn't to blame, but guilt isn't always rational. He was crazy about his sister. He always whispered her name when he talked about her, as though she were . . . I don't know . . . ethereal. He felt as though she sacrificed herself for the family, although, from all objective reports, she must have had a good life. Taggart doted on her, and there's nothing to suggest she wasn't happy."

Caroline scanned the kitchen. An impressive assortment of pots and pans hung above a sturdy work island. Glass-fronted storage cabinets lined one wall, with mixing bowls and baking paraphernalia visible through the panes of glass. "Given her background, I suppose it was only natural that Katherine would want her own kitchen." She heaved open the massive door of the huge combination range/oven. "If she did her own baking, she certainly had the oven for it."

"It was state-of-the-art in the late twenties," Jared said. "I had it checked out for safety. It's in great shape. Should be adequate for a tearoom the size I want to open."

"You'll have to get a different consultant for an opinion on that," Caroline said, eyeing the old stove dubiously. "I've done my share of making restaurants look good, but I don't know much about the food-preparation end of the business."

"Can't cook, huh?"

"Not lunch for fifty on an antique stove. That little baby in the corner is more my speed." She nodded toward a microwave oven on a wheeled cart.

Jared chuckled. "A fellow nuker!"

Caroline shrugged playfully. "I may appreciate the beauty and ingenuity of things from a simpler age, but when it comes to real life, give me modern technology and indoor plumbing."

"I'm beginning to like you," Jared said jauntily. The easy rapport between them made it seem perfectly natural that he should cup her elbow to guide her out of the kitchen when they resumed the tour of the house. She seemed at ease with the small intimacy and made no move to pull away.

They returned to the Grand Salon and entered the room in front of the kitchen. "This was Taggart's room," he told Caroline. "The doors at either end of the back wall lead to the bathroom, and into a walk-in closet. Both of them butt against the kitchen wall and were added when Taggart moved downstairs. Most of the furnishings are original."

"I remember reading somewhere that king-size water beds were big in the thirties," Caroline said drolly.

"I said 'most,'" Jared reminded. "My quest for authenticity doesn't stretch to sleeping on an ancient hospital bed."

"You're living here?"

"For the time being. I needed a place to hang my hat for a while, and this old house was just sitting here empty."

"Katherine House is some hat rack," Caroline remarked, stooping to examine the Oriental rug centered on the floor.

"Beats moving in with Mom and Dad," Jared said.

Caroline was testing the nap of the carpet with her fingertips. "Do you know how many decorators would *kill* to find a rug like this for their discriminating clients?"

"Don't tell me. I might lie awake at night worrying that someone's going to throttle me in my sleep."

"I wasn't speaking literally. It *is* a beautiful carpet, though. And a beautiful table, and a beautiful lamp, and—"

"You really get into your work, don't you?"

"On some jobs," she said, rising. She smiled wryly. "Maybe I shouldn't tell you this before we've put figures on a contract, but I've always been fascinated by Katherine House."

The lady-killer smile flashed again. "Then let me show you my parlor," he said suggestively, and led her into the next of the row of rooms that opened off the Grand Salon. "This was the library. I use it as a den."

A television and a contemporary, overstuffed leather chair with matching ottoman blended with the turn-of-the-century furnishings surprisingly well. A newspaper and coffee mug on the table beside the chair gave the room a lived-in look, an intimate atmosphere. Caroline was drawn to the massive fireplace with its carved mantel, and she slid her forefinger along a groove in the carving.

"Do you always touch things you admire?" Jared asked. He hadn't meant the question to sound suggestive, but as it emerged, his mind raced with possibilities of areas she might touch if she admired *him*.

"I'm a very tactile person," she said. "Some decorators are partial to color or lines. I like texture."

Her sultry voice glided over his senses with the sinuousness of a satin nightie floating to the floor. She had answered calmly, but as their gazes met, he caught the awareness in the depths of her eyes.

Jared Colin was an imposing male presence—tall, lean and virile; so clean he squeaked and so handsome he sparkled. But Katherine House was a dream assignment, the job of a lifetime, and she wasn't about to let sexual chemistry mess it up for her. They were going to be working in close quarters, especially since he was living in Katherine House, so she was going to have to be careful to keep their relationship on a cordial, professional level.

Caroline turned her attention back to the mantel. "It's cedar, isn't it?"

"Yes," Jared said. "There are six fireplaces, and all the mantels are cedar."

He'd converted the front parlor into an office, creating an intriguing blend of old and new with a massive oak desk that faced out to visitors and a sleek computer grouping at a utilitarian contemporary desk facing the wall. A peculiar five-paneled turret with high windows jutted out at the corner, just large enough for a rocking chair. Jared had filled it with plants instead. A basket of ivy hung from the peak of the small turret, and leafy tendrils trailed down like green ribbons to tickle the tops of a variety of potted plants set in, on and around a grouping of torchères and jardinières.

"Did all these come from the house?" she asked, referring to the antique candle and plant stands.

"I found them in one of the rooms upstairs, along with an old sewing machine and one of those dress dummies. There's stuff everywhere. I was hoping, considering how offbeat this job is anyway, that when we got down to discussing terms, you'd agree to do a little sorting and cataloging."

Caroline's eyes twinkled with excitement. "It's going to be like going through a treasure chest."

"More like a dusty old attic," Jared warned.

"Lead the way," Caroline said enthusiastically. "I'm a sucker for dusty old attics."

"If you keep up this negotiating strategy, you're going to wind up paying me to give you this job."

Caroline tilted her head and smiled sweetly. "A nice man like you wouldn't possibly take advantage of me." *Especially with the threat of Aunt Essie finding out hanging over his head!*

"Maybe not in business," Jared muttered under his breath as she preceded him out of the room. But as he watched her inspect the detail work in one of the ornamental gingerbread arches beneath the stairway, his mind played with distinctly nonbusiness situations in which he might be sorely tempted to press his advantage. Her enthusiasm was refreshing—and her legs were good enough to make a mature man drool.

"Rosewood?" she asked, with a querying lift of an eyebrow.

Jared nodded. "So's the wainscoting around the ceiling." With a broad gesture he extended his arm toward the stairway. "Shall we?"

The stairs were narrow enough to necessitate ascending single file. Caroline took her time, stopping along the way to exclaim over the hand-blown glass in the window at the first landing and feel the texture of the aged wallpaper along the wall that led up the final bank of steps to the second floor. Jared watched her, taking proprietary pleasure in her fascination and appreciation of his house. He also derived a bit of pleasure from noticing the way her tailored shorts hugged her bottom as she mounted a step, and the way her hair shimmered when the sunlight hit it.

At the second story, the stairway opened into a large central hallway. There were doors, one each, in the side walls, and two doors in the wall facing the stairs. "Bedrooms," Jared said. "And this central hall will be a lounge area where guests can mingle, or whatever."

"Which is the room with the sewing machine?" Caroline asked, ready for a preview glimpse of what she was in for.

"Why don't we go up to the cupola first—save this floor for last?" Jared suggested abruptly.

There was command in the suggestion, and Caroline sensed a sudden tension in him, as though the thought of her going into the rooms on this floor made him uncomfortable for some reason. She wondered what could make him apprehensive, especially when he'd been so blasé about parading her through his personal rooms downstairs, water bed and all.

The prospect of seeing the Kaleidoscope Room, however, was too irresistible to leave her pondering over the mystery of his attitude. "Do patches of colored sunlight really dance on the floor?" she asked, as she bounded up the narrow wooden stairway toward the cupola.

Jared laughed, partly at the whimsical notion, and partly out of joy derived from her exuberance. "I suppose that's one way of describing it."

It took only seconds to mount the stairs. Caroline reached the narrow landing and attempted to open the door, without results. "Either it's locked or it's stuck," she reported, as Jared reached the top step.

"Stuck, most likely," Jared said. "I don't remember locking it. Here, let me try."

He reached around her to work with the stubborn lock. Even though he was on the step below her, his height surpassed hers. Caroline felt the warmth of his body near hers—that radiant heat peculiar to men—and recognized the scent of the classic shaving soap her grandfather had always used. Despite her resolve to keep their interaction purely professional, she would have been disinclined to discourage him if he'd slipped his arms around her waist and hugged her, maybe rested his chin on her shoulder and pressed his cheek against hers. Her imagination had progressed to the gentlest of fantasy kisses when the door yielded with a groan and a creak.

"I'm going to bring some oil up here for these hinges," Jared said, but Caroline scarcely heard as she stared past him for her first real look at the Kaleidoscope Room. A shiver crawled along her spine. At first, Caroline attributed the chill to the excitement she felt at finally seeing the room that had inspired her childhood daydreams. But what she was experiencing wasn't a pleasant feeling of anticipation—rather, it was a decidedly unpleasant, foreboding sensation.

"Aren't you going in?"

Jared's voice shattered the spell of whatever had taken her in its thrall. Almost as though snapping out of a deep trance, Caroline replied, "Yes, of course," and entered the room.

It was as breathtaking as she'd always envisioned it. The afternoon sun gave life to the stained-glass designs set into the domed ceiling, so that the flowers in the motifs seemed to be blowing in a meadow breeze. Spots of color did indeed dance over the floor, and over the pale sheets of muslin that had been draped over the furniture to protect it. Dust motes raised by the infusion of air from the opening of the door hung in the air like flurrying snowflakes, creating a three-dimensional impressionistic image of the rays of colored light projecting through the windows.

Along the walls there were numerous ordinary windows, each one square with four panes of clear glass. "The light in this room is fantastic," Caroline said. "I hadn't realized there would be clear glass windows, too." They weren't visible from the street.

"Designed for cross ventilation in Florida's hot summers," Jared told her. "A third-story room could get pretty warm in the days before air-conditioning. If I can remember which ones to open, we can get some air in here."

Built-in window seats lined the walls beneath the windows. Jared braced a knee on them as he leaned forward to wrestle open a window on each side of the room. The two windows provided a surprising amount of ventilation, immediately alleviating the mustiness of the stale air.

"According to the legend, no one was allowed up here once Taggart moved downstairs," Jared said. "But the couple he kept as housekeeper and handyman must have done some maintenance through the years, or everything would be in much worse shape up here. It must have been a matter of them sneaking upstairs and his pretending not to notice."

"Small intrigues," Caroline observed.

"You *are* an incurable romantic," Jared said. "Taggart had made his statement by moving downstairs, but deep down inside he probably balked at letting the house deteriorate around him in a Dickinsonian gesture of grief."

"Amazing!"

"What is?"

"Nothing," she answered with a sigh. "I just remembered it was his wife you were related to, not Taggart. I guess it isn't so amazing that you could turn out to be such a cynic, when he obviously was a romantic at heart."

"I have my romantic moments," Jared said, with that lady-killer smile.

"I'll just bet you do," she countered wryly. She would have bet her cat's ninth life that he'd been a ladies' man before most of the boys his age had been willing to admit girls weren't just pains in the neck.

"You wound my heart with your attitude," he said.

Your ego, maybe. Your heart, fat chance! Caroline thought. She said, with a notable lack of sympathy, "I suspect you'll survive a bit of skepticism."

Jared answered with a benign harrumph, and they fell into a comfortable silence while Caroline made a cursory circuit of the room, lifting the corners of the muslin dust protectors to check out the furniture.

"You'll have to look at each piece and see which should be salvaged, and which should be tossed," Jared said.

"'Tossing' anything in this room would be blasphemy," Caroline replied. "That chaise longue could probably get by with just a professional shampooing for the present. It's easy to see why this was Katherine Taggart's favorite room."

"There was an old Victrola record player with a horn-shaped speaker on that corner cabinet. I took it to a specialist in Orlando to be cleaned and oiled. He says it's in excellent condition, considering. Katherine used to spend hours in here listening to her music."

"Are there old records?" Caroline asked.

"An entire drawerful of them. We'll see if any of them are still playable when we get the Victrola back. If not, we'll order some."

"What do you plan to do with this room?"

"Besides restore it as closely as possible to the way it was when Katherine spent so much time here, I'm not sure. It might make a great special-events room, but there are some problems."

"Accessibility," Caroline prompted.

Jared nodded. "Those steep stairs are a problem, and handicap access would be extremely difficult. We'd have to get an access exemption for the upper floors. Food and beverages would have to be carted up manually, and we'd have people trooping up and down stairs to use the second-floor powder room."

"You've clearly given this quite a bit of thought."

"And I keep reaching the conclusion that the best course of action is just to restore the room and let anyone who wants to see it, see it. We wouldn't officially offer it as a public meeting room, but if someone requested it—"

"You could suggest that the tearoom would cater a private party. Very clever."

"Just common sense," Jared said, and then, after several indrawn breaths and a succession of peculiar grimaces, he sneezed heartily.

Hark! Signs of human frailty! "*Gesundheit!*" Caroline said.

"It's the dust," Jared explained. "We're going to have to get a cleaning team up here, now that you're here to supervise. For the time being, why don't we check out the second floor? It's not quite as du-du-dusty!"

"*Gesundheit!*" Caroline said again. "What about the windows?"

"Leave them open, let in some air. I'll close them later."

Caroline paused for one long, lingering look at the patches of color dancing on the wood floor before following him down the stairs.

He hadn't exaggerated about the storage room being full. Feeling as though she'd been miniaturized and thrown into a toy box reserved for dollhouse furnishings, Caroline wove her way through the hodgepodge of old furniture and bric-a-brac in order to get a general idea of what was stored there. Wedged between a hip-high dresser and a thigh-high steamer trunk, she paused to examine the drawer pulls on the dresser.

"These are porcelain and brass," she said. "They'll be gorgeous when they're polished up."

"Maybe we can use that piece in one of the guest bedrooms," Jared said. He was standing just inside the door, hands in his pockets, watching her intently, but not really involved with the antiques—at least, not with the kind of emotional involvement true devotees pour into beautiful artifacts of the past. *Could a person who's allergic to dust ever be an antique buff?*

Caroline didn't look up as she asked, "Do you mind if I ask you something . . . well, semipersonal?"

"Not in the least."

"The kind of renovation you're doing is going to be very expensive, and even though you inherited the house and haven't had to invest any capital in mortgages, it's going to be years before you realize any substantial profits—even if your tearoom and inn are eminently successful."

"You want to know why I'm investing so much to yield so little."

She looked at him. "That's the gist of the question."

"You wouldn't buy it if I told you I was committed to the preservation of history and my motives are strictly altruistic?"

Caroline answered with a lift of her eyebrows and a subtle, apologetic shrug of her shoulders.

Jared exhaled wearily. "There's *some* altruism involved. The house is a piece of history, and with so many landmarks being torn down, anyone in a position to maintain one should feel a certain moral imperative to do so."

"Very noble," Caroline said, without condescension.

"And there's the personal angle. Taggart did a lot for my family. If he hadn't built Colin's Breads, my grandfather would never have made it to college or law school, and it's a safe bet that he would never have become governor of Florida. The fact that he *was* governor and owned this house makes Katherine House even more historically significant, but that's less important to me than that he loved this house because it was a link to his sister. I think he *entrusted* it to me instead of willing it to the state with a perpetual maintenance fund because he wanted to keep it linked to the family. I took a look at what I'd inherited and tried to figure the best way to preserve it without turning it into a stuffy museum."

He grinned. "In addition to all of the above, it'll be good for my image as a public-minded citizen to preserve a landmark. Preservation is 'in,' you know, but few people have the ways and means to indulge in it in a big way. I have both."

"Do I hear the beginning rumbles of a political career in the making?"

Jared laughed aloud. "Trust a Bostonian to recognize a politician. Yes, I plan to give it a try. Start out with some grass-roots involvement and see if I can build a solid base for statewide office. I've got the pedigree and the vision. The party people agreed with me that this Katherine House project would be a real asset to my public image."

"I might have known!"

"It's not as though I'm breaking the law or selling out the masses. I'm just exploiting an exploitable asset."

Caroline's expression revealed her skepticism.

"Hey," Jared said defensively, "I'm nobody's pawn. The image consultants drooled over the idea of my renovating Katherine House, but it was my idea. They gave me a whole list of suggestions about how to beef up my image, but I don't kowtow. I take their recommendations or leave them according to what seems right for me."

Caroline dropped the muslin drape she'd been peeping under to look directly at Jared. "Indulge my curiosity— What kind of suggestions do image consultants give aspiring politicians?"

"They told me to get out of Tallahassee, for starters. I kind of lingered there after finishing up at Florida State. But there are too many politicians, and too much activity there for someone trying to break in. Once I decided to establish a residency base somewhere else, Katherine House seemed like the logical place to come. After all, it's home."

"Your family's here?"

"About twenty miles up the road. My dad's CEO of Colin's Breads."

"I see," Caroline said thoughtfully. After a pause, she asked, "So what advice did they give you that you aren't following?"

"They said I should tone down my wardrobe a bit. Narrower stripes."

"You're a rebel, all right," she agreed, eyeing his awning-stripe shirt.

"My shirt is a small rebellion," Jared said. "I'm just establishing my own style."

"Umm. And what larger rebellions are you committing?"

"The biggie is that I haven't gotten married."

4

"MARRIED?" CAROLINE SAID.

"To the proper woman, of course. A good wife is an asset, and a bachelor existence, a distinct liability. That's a direct quote."

Caroline rested her fists on her waist. "That's the most sexist propaganda I've ever heard."

"It makes some sense, at least to them. Being unmarried leaves me vulnerable to gossip. If I have an active social life, see lots of women, I'm a playboy, and everyone knows what an unstable lot *they* are."

"I shudder to think about the harm *bachelor* politicians could do this country."

"And if I live quietly and keep my social life discreet, there's always the chance that my sexual orientation might come into question. So I'm damned if I date, and damned if I don't."

"So you're supposed to find some suitable little woman to stand by her man."

"That was the suggestion."

Caroline laughed unexpectedly—a rich, throaty laugh that resounded with sincerity.

"I don't know what you find so amusing," Jared said.

"It's more pathetic than amusing, but it occurred to me— Did you mention this to Aunt Essie?"

"Ye gods, no! And don't you dare, either!"

"Why not? You'd have the most active social life in the history of the state."

Jared knew she was teasing him, but the very prospect of getting Aunt Essie involved in his personal life terrified him.

"Every woman in the society would be dropping by with their visiting granddaughters or great-nieces. Your tearoom business would boom."

"Caroline—"

"And the dinner invitations—" she pressed. "Just think of—"

"We've still got some rooms to go through," he interjected desperately.

"I didn't know we were in a hurry," she said, with an infuriated bit of sarcasm.

"We're not. It's just—" He sniffed in exasperation, then snapped, "One word about that stupid recommendation to Aunt Essie and you're fired!"

It was too strong, and he immediately felt foolish for having overreacted—even more so when Caroline clicked her heels together, saluted and barked, with the intensity of a marine in training, "Yes, sir."

Jared shoved his hands in his pockets and frowned, looking, Caroline thought, like a frustrated little boy being made to go to Sunday school when he'd rather be playing baseball.

"It would be unendurable," he said.

"Lighten up, Colin. Your secret's safe with me."

"If Aunt Essie got it in her head to matchmake—"

"Don't worry about it! Now that I've seen this room, I wouldn't jeopardize this job over anything as silly as some advice from an image consultant."

A charged silence followed. Finally Caroline turned her attention to the lace trim on the bodice of the dress on the dressmaker's dummy. "Nice," she announced. "This wasn't some parlor maid's home sewing—I'll bet it was being made for your Great-Aunt Katherine."

"I wouldn't know," Jared said.

"If this dress was for her, then this dummy must have been adjusted to her size. She had a nice figure, didn't she?"

"I guess. It's a little hard to tell from a dummy."

"Umm," Caroline said distractedly. "You know, if we were very careful, we could take this dress off and dry-clean it, maybe display it on the dummy. It would be a nice touch. Authentic, and a bit unusual."

"You're the decorator."

"As long as I keep your secret," Caroline said wryly.

Jared scowled, but either she didn't notice, or she deliberately ignored his displeasure. Jared suspected the latter when she said, "I don't know why you're so sensitive about that advice, anyway."

"I'm not sensitive about it. I just don't want it spread all over town that I'm looking for a wife."

"Are you?"

"Of course not!"

"I don't know why not. It makes a lot of sense, when you think about it."

"I thought you said it was sexist propaganda."

Caroline shrugged. "From a woman's perspective, it is. But strictly from your point of view, the right marriage could be advantageous. For instance, if you were married to the right woman, you might have saved yourself the expense of a decorator."

"But you'd have missed out on the fun of going through all this junk."

"Well, then, I'm glad that you didn't take your consultant's advice, because I plan to have a lot of fun with this junk."

Jared relaxed a bit when Caroline discovered a box of trinkets and started sifting through them. He knew she was deliberately goading him—why, he couldn't imagine—but he was irritated out of proportion by her teasing. She was impudent and unpredictable, and he was in imminent danger of losing control of this renovation project if he wasn't very careful. Watching her dig through the trinkets of his great-aunt's era, he thought that he probably should pay her a tidy little severance fee and send her cute little butt back to Boston before he got in over his head. But it really was a cute little butt, and the idea of having her around, sassy mouth and all, was not without appeal.

And then she asked, "What have you got against marriage anyway, Jared?"

"I don't have anything against marriage."

"Humpf!" she sniffed, and the nonword dripped with doubt.

"Marriage is a fine institution," Jared said.

"For other people."

Jared decided that if Ms. Caroline Naylor hadn't driven most of the Eastern Seaboard to restore his house, and if she weren't so enthusiastic about her work and if her hair weren't catching the light from the uncurtained window in a way that made it appear to glow almost like an angel's, he would have fired her on the grounds of sheer perversity. But her hair was catching the light, and though she had a devilish, taunting tongue, her body was the closest thing to heaven he'd seen in months, so he shrugged and said, "For people who want to spend the rest of their lives together."

Cocking her head at an angle that showed her strong chin to advantage, she regarded him with wide eyes and a mischievous grin. "That's a rather romantic notion for a cynic like you."

"I never claimed to be a cynic."

She shook her head the way she would at an exasperating child. "All that stuff about Taggart being a horny old man, and Katherine Taggart being an opportunist—"

"I believe in love, Caroline. I just think it takes a while to establish the kind of foundation necessary for a lifelong commitment."

"No love at first sight?"

"Lust, maybe," he said. "Attraction. Some crazy kind of chemistry based on hormones. Not love."

"So, how do you account for your great-aunt's marriage being so successful?"

"Things were different then. Marriage was forever—no matter why a couple got married. Maybe she and Taggart grew to love each other. Or maybe they were just friends, filling each other's needs. He was rich and lonely. She was poor and beautiful. Their relationship could have been platonic, for all we know."

"I hope not," Caroline said, unconsciously reaching up to ruffle the lace on the bodice of the dummy's dress.

Jared laughed briefly. "What possible difference could it make?"

"It's just such a...sweet story," she said. "It's tragic enough that she died so young. It would be sad if she died without...well, without knowing what it was like to be...to have someone—"

"Umm," Jared said. "I guess it would pop a lot of romantic bubbles, at that. Maybe her diaries will—"

"She left *diaries?*" Caroline exclaimed, twirling to face him.

"We found them on the desk upstairs," he replied. "I brought them downstairs and dusted them off. The few entries I've read don't seem intensely personal, but they seem to have a great deal of detail of daily life of the period. I was thinking of having them typeset and bound, to sell in the tearoom. Maybe you'd like to read them."

"You know I would," she said.

"Good. I'd like your opinion."

"Really?" she asked, making it sound like a farfetched concept. She was digging in the gadget box again.

He grinned. "On the diary."

Caroline picked up something that could have come from the kitchen, eyed it skeptically, replaced it in the box and dusted her hands together.

"With the dollar tour, you get authentic grit," Jared reminded.

"It's endemic in old houses," she said. "I brought some old work clothes." She faced Jared. "I've got a general idea what's here, if you're ready to go on with that dollar tour."

The next two bedrooms contained bedsteads without mattresses, a spartan sprinkling of tables and chests, and a couple of table lamps with promising bases and unsalvageable shades. The bathrooms, added to the house when indoor plumbing became feasible, were nondescript in design, but the fixtures were in fairly good condition, and Caroline commented that it would be interesting working around the original fixtures, particularly the claw-footed bathtubs, although the toilets might have to be replaced, and the mirrors required resilvering.

The last door off the wide central hall was closed, and Jared paused with his hand on the knob, as though reluctant to open it. "There's a reason I saved this room until last," he said.

"It's the master suite, the room Katherine and Samuel Taggart shared?" Caroline ventured. Jared nodded, then exhaled heavily, warily. He still seemed reluctant to open the door, and Caroline was puzzled by his attitude. Why was he stalling? He certainly wasn't the type to get emotionally overwrought over entering the bedroom of a long-dead relative he'd never met.

Seconds passed, and still he stood with his hand on the knob without twisting it. "Jared?" Caroline prompted.

He opened the door and gestured for her to enter ahead of him. It was a huge room, with a fireplace and large windows. The massive tester bed was properly made-up and covered by a quilted comforter. The room had been thoroughly cleaned, the walls stripped smooth and the floors and furniture waxed to a warm luster. There was an Oriental rug, similar to the one Caroline had admired in Jared's quarters.

On top of the oak chest of drawers, centered on a freshly laundered crocheted table scarf, was a huge basket of cut flowers. The colorful arrangement stood out in the room like a cranberry stain on a white tablecloth, and Caroline walked over for a closer look. Even if there had been no card inserted among the blossoms on a plastic pick, the variety of flowers, symmetry of the arrangement and perfect fern fronds used as filler made it obvious that the bouquet had come from a floral shop.

"Cookie Naylor" was written on the tiny envelope. Caroline glanced at Jared briefly before removing the envelope from the pick.

"Caroline," Jared said, catching her hands in his before she could take out the card. She looked up at him expectantly, mystified by his hesitance and the abrupt gesture.

After meeting her eyes, he exhaled a defeated sigh and released her hands. "You're not...what I had expected," he said.

Caroline didn't know how to respond to such a statement, or even if a response was necessary.

"Aunt Essie didn't say... I thought you'd be ... *different. Older. More—*"

"Are you firing me?" she asked.

"No! I mean...no. You're enthusiastic, and I'm sure you'll do an excellent job. I just didn't know... I didn't plan—"

"Maybe I'd better take a look at this card." She took the card from the envelope, skimmed over it, then read aloud. "'Welcome to Taggartville and Katherine House'?"

It seemed innocuous enough—certainly nothing to make a man like Jared Colin behave as self-consciously as a timid schoolboy.

He said, "When you asked me to provide a place to stay, I didn't think it would be a problem. But in the winter, with all the snowbirds, and with a cat—"

"You *did* find a place?" Caroline asked.

"*Found* may not be the best word."

"What exactly would the best word be?"

"*Made?*"

Realization dawned. Caroline raised her eyebrows in question and made a sweeping gesture with her hand to indicate the room.

Jared nodded, then said, "Look, Caroline, if you're uncomfortable with this—"

"It looks . . . habitable," Caroline said.

"Of course, it's habitable! The mattress and springs are new, and it's been cleaned, and there's a private bath. I even put in a phone jack."

"Then what's the problem?" Caroline asked.

"This isn't Boston, Caroline."

Caroline gave him an exasperated frown. "I knew that when I took the job. I told you, I live simply. If the bed's comfortable and there's a private bath—"

"Caroline," he said, spreading the name into three syllables as though trying to make a point with a slow-witted child, "I live downstairs, and you—" He drove his fingers through his hair, then exhaled. "You're . . . well, young and attractive, and—"

Caroline batted her eyelashes, feigning innocence, perversely enjoying his discomfort. "Why, Jared, are you afraid you might succumb to passion and come up and have your way with me?"

"Certainly not. But there could be—"

"Because if you did, well, mercy me, I'd just have to tell everyone how you compromised me, and then you'd have to marry me."

"Would you be serious, please? In a town the size of Taggartville there could be talk. If you're in any way uncomfortable about this, we can make other arrangements."

"I thought you'd tried."

~ "I did. The residence hotels were full. Aunt Essie has a friend with a spare room, but she's allergic to cats. So, I thought—"

"And quite rightly," Caroline said. "It makes perfect sense. Think of the time I'll save not having to commute. And the convenience of being *en place*—not to mention the money you'll save by not having to pay rent to someone else."

"I didn't set this up because I'm cheap!"

"I didn't say you did! Look, Jared, it's a great idea. And if you're worried about my reputation, don't bother. I'm only going to be here a few weeks, and I don't give a damn what the gossipmongers say. Every native in town probably already knows we had cobbler together at the Cow Café today, anyway."

"That's not exactly on the level of *living together*."

"Living on separate floors in the same house is not living *together*."

"That's a distinction the gossipmongers will fail to see."

"Answer one question for me, will you, Jared?"

Jared gave her a grudging nod, and she asked, "Whose reputation are you really worried about—yours or mine?"

"What kind of question is that?"

"It's a very simple question. Taggartville is a fishbowl, and even though we both have ties here, we're both exotic outsiders. You're the governor's grandson, and I'm a big-city decorator. We're both single, and we're going to be spending a lot of time together in Katherine House. I'll be going back to Boston in a few weeks, so I could care less what the Taggartville gossip mill churns out. But you're going to be living here, and you're launching a political career, so if you're concerned, I'll respect that concern."

Jared considered her point a moment, then smiled. "I think my reputation will withstand a little gossip—if you're sure you're comfortable with the situation."

She cocked her head at a coquettish angle. "You're absolutely sure you won't get swept up on the wings of passion and come stealing up the stairs in the dead of night to ravish me?"

"If I do," he said wryly, "the worst that can happen is that I'll do the honorable thing afterward and make my image consultants very happy."

Caroline scowled. Jared continued. "Don't be modest, Miz Naylor. I read your résumé. Master's degree in art history from a prestigious school. Summer volunteer work at a prestigious art museum. Internship at a prestigious design firm. You speak French—"

"And I thought sending you my résumé was just a formality."

"I don't know why I didn't notice it immediately," Jared pressed on, enjoying himself. "You've got Florida First Lady stamped on your forehead. You've got the right background, just the right look. Sleek and blond. Classy, but benign. Approachable. You love animals. You've got a nickname—"

"No one's called me Cookie in years."

"Doesn't matter! Nicknames make good copy. Cookie—the media would eat it up—no pun intended, of course."

"Of course," Caroline snapped.

Jared was on a roll. "Think about it: Ladybird Johnson. Happy Rockefeller. Mo Dean."

"She wound up visiting her husband in prison, didn't she?"

"Face it, Cookie, you'd be the perfect political wife."

"A fate worse than death!" Caroline declared. "If that door doesn't have a lock, I'm installing one!"

Jared laughed. "Does that mean you're staying?"

Caroline shrugged. "Why not? I've got a 'watchcat' to protect me." She looked around the room and through the door, into the wide hallway. "Dessie's going to go crazy with all these rooms and all this stuff to explore."

"Maybe she'll catch a few mice. I've heard some scurrying around at night."

Caroline gave him an exasperated frown. "Thanks for sharing that with me, Jared. Now I'll sleep well."

He gave her one of his lady-killer smiles. "All you have to do is call and I'll come up to rescue you."

"Oh, no!" Caroline said. "If any mouse shows up in my room, I'll throw a shoe at it, thank you. I'm not going to risk inciting you to uncontrollable passion and ending up first lady of Florida."

And you might just be the one who could do it, Jared thought, suddenly suffering visions of her in a slinky nightgown, with her blond hair loose around her face and her feet bare. Talk was easily dealt with—but how was he supposed to sleep knowing she was just above him, nearly naked and snuggled under the covers in a bed he owned?

"I'll bring up your bags so you can get settled," he volunteered, desperate for something active to do.

Caroline nodded. "Good idea. Then I can let Dessie out to explore. She's probably going stir-crazy in that carrier."

A few minutes later, all of Caroline's luggage and the assorted paraphernalia necessary for the care and feeding of a cat were clustered in the middle of the floor of her new room. Jared tactfully excused himself, saying he had some work to catch up with in his office, and that she should let him know if she needed anything.

Caroline watched him leave and listened to his footsteps grow more distant as he descended the stairs before hissing a whispered, "Yes-s-s-s!" and doing a run-in-place dance—on tiptoe so as not to be heard on the floor below. Living in Katherine House! The physical manifestation of her fondest dream! The rosewood floors, the wainscoting, the furniture! The cedar mantels, the stained-glass cupola, the storage room filled with hardwood floors and porcelain-and-brass drawer pulls! Oriental rugs, windows with blown-glass panes, claw-footed bathtubs! She was the proverbial dog in a smoke-house, kid in the candy store, baseball fanatic at the final game of the World Series. Katherine House was a mirror into the past, a smorgasbord of period furnishing, and she was living there, a part of it, sleeping where Katherine and Samuel Taggart had slept, touching the things they'd touched.

She sat on the edge of the bed and traced the rows of tiny stitches that traced scallops on the comforter, awed by the incalculable in-and-out thrusts of the needle required to create the scallops, the skill and patience represented in those aged strands of cotton thread. A week ago she'd been hemmed in by the bleakest of winters, trapped in projects that had grown oppressively repetitive. It seemed almost inconceivable that such a short time later she could be in Taggartville, living in and working in the mansion that had so captured her imagination in her youth. And she wasn't even going to think about the added bonus of working with a man like Jared Colin.

Jared Colin, grandson of a governor. She'd been expecting a stuffed-shirt conservative, but she'd gotten two-and-one-half-inch awning stripes over hard sinew instead. Lord, but he was beautiful. He knew it, of course. And he was spoiled rotten. But he had a sense of humor and he didn't take himself too seriously, and he was considerate and pleasant enough to talk to. If she had to share a house with a man, sharing a house with a man as charming as Jared Colin held a lot of appeal.

She slapped the tops of her thighs in a gesture of resolve. This sitting around thinking about Jared Colin wasn't getting anything accomplished. She had a litter box to set up, food and water dishes to fill, and a furry roommate to introduce to her new environment. She unpacked all the things she'd brought to make Desdemona feel at home—the Purrfect place mat on which Desdemona's dishes were always set, the flannel catnip mouse that Dessie loved to bat about with her paws. She chuckled at this; Dessie was used to carpets—wait until she saw how her mouse would slide over polished wood.

After she'd filled the food and water dishes, she went downstairs to fetch Desdemona. The front door was still propped open. Jared was in his office, seated at his desk, talking on the phone. He smiled and waved, and she waved back before picking up Desdemona's carrier. She spoke softly, reassuringly to the cat as she mounted the stairs, chatting about a new place to live. Desdemona was docile, as she always was on those rare occasions when she was confined to the carrier.

At first, Caroline didn't recognize the sound as coming from Desdemona. It began as a low hum, like a mechanical whir; and being in a strange house, Caroline's initial thought was that it was a fan or pump or vibrating pipe. But the sound swelled with each step up the stairway, growing loud and feral, until it was impossible not to realize it was coming from the cat carrier. By the time they reached the second-floor hallway, it had escalated into a savage shriek, the piercing feline equivalent of a primal scream.

Caroline set the carrier down and sat on the floor next to it, cooing endearments to Desdemona and debating whether to open the door and try to cuddle her. She was startled to discover Jared on the top step, winded and looking as though he'd been scared out of a year's growth; it would have been impossible to hear his footsteps on the stairs above the din of Desdemona's cry.

"I thought *you* were screaming," he shouted, with a touch of the irritation that comes in the aftermath of unfounded fear.

Caroline shrugged her shoulders to indicate helplessness. "She's *never* done this. The traveling must have upset her."

In desperation, Caroline opened the door of the carrier. Dessie was crouched in the rear corner, hair standing on end, tail plumped like a caterpillar on growth hormones. The scream had contracted to a hoarse growl, but menacing in its intensity. "Dessie," Caroline said sticking her hand in to caress her. "Poor Dessie, it's all—"

Caroline yelped in pain and jerked her hand out of the carrier. Stunned, she stared from it to Jared's face, shocked that Desdemona had scratched *her.*

"She's upset," Jared said.

Caroline stood abruptly and reached for the carrier. Jared beat her to the handle. "Where do you want her?"

"My room," Caroline replied, her voice tense.

She closed the door behind them once they were in the room and showed Jared Desdemona's dishes. "Put her down here and open the hatch. Maybe she'll calm down and venture out if she smells her food, or sees the mat."

Jared did as she asked, but the cat showed no signs of leaving the carrier. He looked at Caroline. "You've got to take care of that scratch."

Caroline was trembling. "I've got some antibiotic cream in my makeup kit," she said, and walked away, disappearing into the bathroom.

She'd left the door open. Jared heard water running in the sink, and debated whether to follow her. He couldn't slough off the image of her, so betrayed by the cat's aggression, trembling, the stricken expression in her eyes more disturbing than the beads of blood oozing from the scratches on her hand.

She was just cutting off the tap when he rounded the corner into the bathroom. Closing her eyes, she exhaled a ragged breath, then opened her eyes and gave him a sardonic look before reaching for the tube of antibiotic.

"Here," he said, reaching for the tube at the same time. "Let me help."

"It probably won't sting as much as the soap and water."

"That's not the problem," Jared said. "You're shaking."

She dropped her left hand and docilely allowed him to lift her injured hand, then stared stoically as he spread the cream over the scratches.

"All done," he said.

She nodded without looking at him. Her dejection made her seem vulnerable, small and defenseless. Jared could smell her cologne, a light, subtle scent with an undertone of sandalwood. He couldn't just let her stand there, so alone, when she was so close, and it was so easy to comfort her. He stretched his arm across her drooping shoulders and pulled her against him. He felt her shudder, then relax. Gradually she turned, slipping her arms around his waist, accepting the human comfort he offered for what it was.

"She was upset by the trip," he said.

"I know," Caroline said. "It's just so unlike her."

"She scared the doowaddly out of me," he said.

Already, their embrace was loosening, and they were moving apart.

"She's never made a sound like that before. Never." Her arms were no longer around him, but hanging limply at her sides. "Maybe it was the stairs. The carrier may have swung or tilted on the way up."

"Sounds reasonable to me." They'd both moved, putting a small but significant distance between them with nearly imperceptible steps.

Caroline looked up at him then, and their gazes locked, sparking sudden sexual recognition. The urge to tilt her head back, inviting him to kiss her was strong, but Caroline looked away instead.

Jared was her employer, and she was going to be living in the same house with him, and she realized that kissing wasn't wise.

Jared was relieved when Caroline looked away. She was his employee, and he was far too attracted to her, and living in the same house with her was going to be difficult enough without his knowing what it was like to kiss her.

So, instead of kissing her, Jared lifted her injured hand and examined it critically. "This ought to be covered. I've got some gauze downstairs."

Caroline went with him downstairs and submitted to first aid remembered from Boy Scout training, thanked him graciously, and then returned to her room, alone, where she was greeted by a familiar crackling noise: the sound of Desdemona's teeth contentedly pulverizing her dry cat food.

"Well, *bon appétit*," Caroline said sarcastically, slamming the door shut behind her. Desdemona paused long enough to give Caroline a look of feline hauteur, then resumed her meal.

"Ingrate!" Caroline murmured, but that night, after having conducted a thorough exploration of Caroline's room, the closet and the bathroom, Dessie leaped atop the quilted comforter and dropped her flannel mouse on Caroline's chest, then thrust her nose in Caroline's face, meowing persistently.

"Oh," Caroline said, "so now you want to make up! I suppose you expect me to pet you, too." There was more nudging, and another meow, indignant this time. Caroline laughed, and took her hand out from under the covers so she could scratch Desdemona behind the ears. "Oh, all right! I forgive you. I forgive you."

Soon Dessie was stretched on her back, purring, while Caroline rubbed her snowy white chest. "I suppose I should be grateful to you, anyway. If it weren't for you, I'd be living in Aunt Essie's friend's spare room instead of sleeping in Katherine Taggart's tester bed."

5

WHETHER IT WAS THE CHARM of Katherine House or the rigors of two and a half days on the road and two nights in strange hotels—Caroline suspected the latter—she slept well in Katherine Taggart's bed on her first night in Katherine House. She awoke to the sound of cat food being crackled by cat's teeth—a sound as familiar as an old alarm clock, since Desdemona always stuffed herself in the mornings.

The sound night's sleep, the bright sunlight filtering through the boughs of the magnolia tree outside the window, so different from the soggy daylight of the winter she'd left behind her, and the thoughts of work that permitted creativity as well as performance filled her with energy. She dressed and bounded down the stairs to check the pantry for breakfast fare, since Jared had assured her she would have full run of the kitchen.

She was hoping for Raisin Bran cereal, but found Jared instead, as sharp looking as the day before in charcoal-gray slacks, a salmon-colored oxford shirt, and suspenders. He was raiding a box of Colin's Breads Danish pastries, which he shoved across the table with the invitation to help herself. "Coffee's made, too, and there's orange juice in the refrigerator."

Raisin Bran lost its appeal in the face of a cheese Danish. Caroline poured herself a glass of orange juice and then sat down opposite Jared at the table near the window just as Jared was reaching into the box for his second pastry.

"How's your hand?" Jared asked.

"Healing nicely." She'd replaced the loose gauze wrap with a strategically placed Band-Aid strip that would keep the deepest part of the scratch clean.

"And the perpetrator?"

"Back to her sweet normal self. She brought me her stuffed mouse as a peace offering and slept with me last night."

Caroline could have bitten her tongue off the instant the words were out of her mouth. They were both trying very hard to ignore the chemistry between them, but the reality of the embrace they'd shared and the kiss-that-could-have-been was there between them, insistent and undeniable; if they expected to maintain the precarious balance between awareness and denial, she was going to have to avoid incendiary phrases—phrases like *slept with me*.

She looked at Jared, hoping to see that he hadn't noticed the potential innuendo. But he was grinning, and his grin, while friendly, was too warm for simple friendship. "A stuffed mouse, huh?" he said. "I'll have to remember that the next time I'm trying to impress a cat lover."

"It only works if it's the cat's favorite toy," she said smugly. She didn't know why, but his casual reference to seducing other women annoyed her more than it should have.

"Too bad."

"So many cat lovers, so few sure things," she said drolly.

Jared abandoned his Danish to go to the coffeemaker. He held up the glass pot. "Coffee?"

"No, thanks."

"Sure? We could stir in some sugar. It might sweeten your disposition."

She couldn't resist returning his teasing smile. "I'll stick to orange juice."

"Suit yourself. But I'd think you'd want to be wide-awake for the contract negotiations."

"I'm not worried. I've got Aunt Essie as a fail-safe, remember?"

The negotiations took all of ten minutes in Jared's office. Caroline charged reasonable rates, and Jared agreed to them. While he keyed their terms into the computer, Caroline studied the framed diplomas, photographs, certificates of appreciation and awards on his office wall. She stopped in front of the full-color cover of a magazine called *Today's Florida Business*. There, wearing pin-striped dress pants, white shirt, flowered tie, suspenders and white oxfords, was Jared, posing with four men about his age, each of whom appeared to be just as cocky and self-assured as Jared. Each of the men was dressed in a distinct style—one in jeans, chambray shirt and hard hat; another in yacht captain's gear; a third in surf shorts and tank top; the last in pleated cotton pants and crisply starched sport shirt holding a director's clapper board. White type, reversed against the dark background of the cover shot, labeled them Florida's Young Stallions. The dateline of the magazine showed it to be about a year old.

The computer printer pumped out the finished contract. Jared walked over to Caroline. She arched an eyebrow queryingly. "Florida's Young Stallions?"

"Embarrassing title," he said.

"What's the article about?"

"It follows some of my fraternity buddies and me from graduation. We all seem to have made a mark of some kind."

"What kind of mark?"

"Sam—he's an engineer—started a company, Sammy's Surfatronics, that manufactures surf equipment. Geoff has a charter service that offers cruises with a fantasy theme. Murder mysteries, romance, high roller, pirate voyages— things like that. Larry started his own architectural firm and won all kinds of awards for his energy-efficient-classroom design for a school district down in southern Florida. And Teddy—short for Theodore Cross III—started the production company that made *Fantasy Overload*."

"The movie that was nominated for best picture?"

"Uh-hmm. Made on a shoestring budget of twelve million. Teddy gambled everything he had on it, and directed and produced."

"And what about Jared Colin? What'd he do?"

"Made some interesting investments that paid off. Multiplied my seed money a few times."

"I'd like to read it."

"There's a copy in my files." He got it for her, and she sat down and flipped through it while he collated the copies of the contract that had just rolled out of the printer.

"That explains the headline," Caroline said.

Jared looked up. "What does?"

"This article—it was written by a woman."

Jared sensed the direction she was headed and changed the subject. "The contract's ready for your signature."

"Are you sure I shouldn't read it first, before signing?" Her tone was light.

He answered with the same levity. "Don't you trust me?"

"I don't know. I've never done business with a stallion before."

"Don't even start it," he warned.

"Do you actually *sign* contracts, or do you dip your hoof in ink and leave a print?"

He slid the contract across the desk. "Just sign it." And, handing her a pen, "The standard, human way."

"Yes, sir. Or should that be yes, *sire?*"

The phone rang before Jared could reply. Jared answered it with, "'Lo, Jared Colin," then grew rigid with attention as he listened to the caller.

"Yes, Don. I did call. I heard some new information on that deal we were discussing, and I had a few questions." He rolled his eyes apologetically at Caroline as he listened to the caller again.

Caroline had finished with the contract, and slid it back toward the center of the desk and motioned that she was going upstairs. Jared nodded appreciatively and mouthed, "See you later."

Standing in the middle of the central second-floor hallway, Caroline was suddenly struck by the enormity of the project she'd just signed on for. From where she stood, she could see five doors, four of which were bedrooms, the fifth a bath. Each had to be distinctive, but they all had to fit together. The open hall was wide enough to be furnished as a central lounge for all the guests. And there was the Kaleidoscope Room, which, in keeping with Jared's plan, she wanted to restore as closely as possible to the way it had been when Katherine Taggart was alive. And the dining room downstairs, with tables and tablecloths and something Jared had slipped into the contract called "menu consultation."

She sighed. First things first. She sat down at the table next to the window in her room with a legal pad and made lists—things she had to do, things she needed to get the job done, general impressions, and ideas.

The table needed leveling; it wobbled and creaked as she wrote. Desdemona, who'd been sunning on the windowsill, lifted her head from her paws and cocked it at a quizzical angle.

"It's just a table, Dessie. Old wood groans like old bones," Caroline said soothingly. But the next time she underlined an idea for emphasis, the table protested more loudly than ever. Desdemona flew over Caroline's hands and the legal pad to execute a plop-bottom landing on the bed before diving to the floor and scurrying under the bed, her feet slipping comically on the polished wood floor.

"Still a bit skittish are we?" Caroline asked drolly, then wrote 'Desk/Work station' on her list of immediate needs. No sense driving Desdemona to a nervous collapse. There had been a desk in the storage room, although she couldn't get to it because of all the other furniture. Perhaps after she'd inventoried that room, she could clear a path to it and set up in there.

Having made her lists, Caroline felt she had a more focused perspective on the job she'd agreed to do. Retractable metal tape-measure in one hand, notebook in the other, she left her room to do a systematic tour of the second-floor rooms, measuring width, depth, windows and doors. She made a rough sketch of each room, marking dimensions and making notes around particular details that might be utilized to advantage, or which might need to be played down or camouflaged, and listing needed repairs. Two of the rooms, the master suite included, had dressing rooms that would be converted into closets. The others would require wardrobe cabinets for hanging clothes.

Next came her general impression of each room. "Large windows, good lights—foliage plants? Garden room? Low light—light colors only/could get gloomy. Natural muslin?" In her own suite, she wrote: "Great expanse of wall—use tester bed with draperies as focal point—bridal/anniversary-suite potential? Ask Jared." In the room being used for storage, she wrote simply: "Hopeless until inventoried."

Somewhere along the way, in her room-to-room walking tour, Desdemona had joined her. Caroline had deliberately left the door to her room ajar, leaving the cat the opportunity to explore if she wanted to venture out into more new territory. She padded after Caroline, sniffing floors and furniture, leaping onto windowsills to check out potential nap sites and getting excited over the chirping of unfamiliar birds outside. In the storage room, she circled Caroline's ankles restlessly, caution fighting the natural feline curiosity that Caroline knew would eventually have her poking her nose into every little nook and cranny.

"What's wrong, Dessie?" Caroline asked, leaning over to pet Dessie. "Too much at one time?" She looked around the room—at the furniture wedged together like pieces in a jigsaw puzzle—and sighed. "It *is* daunting, isn't it?" She straightened. "Come on, let's go take a closer look at the Kaleidoscope Room. It's not quite as overwhelming. You can chase the colored lights across the floor."

Desdemona followed her to the bottom step of the stairway and then sat down, staring at the flight of narrow stairs. "Aw, Dessie," Caroline said, pausing halfway up to look down at her. "No guts, no glory. These stairs haven't devoured anybody lately!"

The cat inhaled heavily and puffed out her fur. *If cat's could sigh,* Caroline thought, *that would qualify.* She had reached the top step and was wrestling with the door. They were going to have to get a carpenter in to plane it, she decided, grunting with the strain of tugging on it. It yielded, finally, with a sudden whoosh, and the abrupt lack of resistance almost sent her tumbling down the stairs.

As she stumbled, Desdemona, who'd finally found the courage to venture onto the stairway, let out a piercing wail that faded into a string of agitated hisses and spits. Caroline caught sight of her, back arched, tail fluffed and every hair on end, just before the cat took a flying leap off the steps, made a sliding landing on the wood floor below, spat angrily, and then streaked into Caroline's room.

Having regained her equilibrium, Caroline sat down on the top step, rested her elbows on her knees and her chin on her palms.

She heard Jared's footsteps on the stairs before he reached the second floor and came into view. "Was that a cat that just flew by, or did a dustball from upstairs take life?"

She gave him an exasperated sniff. "Desdemona hasn't adapted to change as well as I'd hoped."

He sat down on the step below her. "You look like a woman who could use lunch at the Cow Café."

"Lunch? It's only—" She consulted her watch, and added, incredulously, "Five after twelve?"

"We must have been busy to lose track of time."

"*We* have been," she said. "I've got several ideas to talk over with you."

He rose, reaching for her hand. "We can talk over the Cow's daily special."

"So," she summarized later, over Mrs. O'Leary's Florida version of shepherd's pie, "I thought I'd ask Aunt Essie if the society members would like to help with the inventory."

"That's an excellent idea. They feel rather proprietary about Katherine House. This would give them some direct involvement with the renovation."

"Some of them may sew or quilt. It'll be very convenient if I can commission local talent to work on draperies or throw pillows. And there are bound to be some antique enthusiasts in the group who can steer me toward the kind of shops and secondhand furniture stores we'll need to tap into for the tearoom."

"Secondhand furniture?" Jared asked.

"Tearooms need a certain ambience," Caroline said, "and personality, some kind of distinctive style. If you order two dozen basic restaurant tables and matching chairs and matching tablecloths, you're going to risk losing the—" she swirled her hands in the air "—the flavor."

"So you think I should . . . ?"

"Buy all kinds of tables, and all kinds of tablecloths and table scarves. And chairs. They don't have to match exactly, so long as they…blend. Make each table unique. You can do the same with your china and flatware. As long as it's good quality, it won't have to match."

"You're the decorator," he said.

"That statement didn't exactly reverberate with enthusiasm."

Jared shrugged. "What do I know about tearooms? That's why I hired you."

After they'd finished their shepherd's pie, Jared ordered cobbler again, but Caroline flatly refused. "Do you eat this way all the time?" she asked.

"Usually. I've got this crazy metabolism. Burns like a funeral pyre."

"It's not fair," she said.

"What's not?"

"That a person should be born rich and good-looking, *and* have an overactive metabolism."

He cocked an eyebrow and conjured one of his lady-killer smiles. "You think I'm good-looking?"

Caroline rolled her eyes in exasperation. "I'm not even going to answer that." *A woman would have to be blind not to think he was good-looking!*

"You do," he said confidently, and after a beat, he grinned and added, "Does this mean my virtue's in jeopardy in the middle of the night?"

"Eat your cobbler!" she retorted, as the waitress set it in front of him.

"I'll have to get in the habit of locking my bedroom door," he said dryly.

"Don't bother. You're not my type."

"Is that a fact?"

"I go for the rugged, macho type."

"Macho?" he repeated.

"Sure," she said. "Cowboys in tight jeans. Motorcycle cops in tall boots. Construction workers with their shirts off, sweating in the sunshine—"

"The ones who whistle at women and shout 'Hey, sugar lips, show us your twin peaks'?"

"Those are the ones," Caroline said, struggling to keep a poker-faced demeanor. She wasn't fooling him, but it pleased her to shake some of that annoying cocksureness of his.

"Uh-hmm," Jared responded. He didn't believe a word of it—not a word—and he couldn't imagine why she was goading him. He finished his cobbler, tossed some bills on the table for a tip and picked up the ticket for the meal to carry it to the cashier. "Come on, Sugar Lips. I've got to make a run into Orlando. I'll drop you at the house on my way out of town."

"Don't count on seeing any twin peaks," Caroline muttered under her breath.

"Did you say something?"

"I said I think I'll call Aunt Essie this afternoon and ask her about getting the society members to help with the inventory."

Aunt Essie was more than enthusiastic at the idea of getting a toehold in the Katherine House renovation, and immediately agreed to recruit and schedule helpers. Caroline thanked her for her cooperation and said she was sure any volunteers she could find would be a great asset to the project.

After changing into a pair of shorts and an old Harvard football jersey left over from her teenage years, Caroline headed for the Kaleidoscope Room. She opened all the windows, creating a strong cross-breeze that ruffled the muslin drapes on the furniture and stirred dust motes into an aerial ballet in the winter sunshine.

Caroline measured and sketched. The windows were all the same size—a plus when it came to designing window treatments. Already her mind was playing with the possibilities—something that would control light and cut down on the greenhouse effect when the air-conditioning was in use, but which would show off to advantage the multipaned windows with their old, imperfect glass. Lines that would complement the circular shape of the room—balloon poufs, perhaps.

She pulled the muslin throws off the window seats to study their construction. The seats appeared to be of rosewood. As she'd expected, when the cushion was removed, the seat itself could be opened, accessing a well of storage space. Caroline smiled, remembering one of her favorite movies, *Arsenic and Old Lace*, and the way bodies were moved in and out of the window seat there: first, one of the "gentlemen" poisoned by the well-intentioned but deadly Brewster sisters, then the unfortunate Mr. Spinalzo, victim of their Frankenstein look-alike nephew, Jonathan. Cary Grant had sat on the seat several times during the movie to keep his aunts, his bride and the police from finding the bodies. What fun a playwright could have in the Kaleidoscope Room with seven window seats!

Caroline sighed. What dreamworld was she living in? Fun? The days of comedic farce were long gone; today they'd make a slasher movie—*Seven Maniacs from Hell*. The maniacs would be members of some strange cult that met in the Kaleidoscope Room to worship the colored lights, and then went out and gathered sacrifices for the stained-glass deity.

She shook off the thought as she knelt to explore the insides of the storage wells. The first held only a crocheted afghan, undoubtedly called into service as a lap robe on chilly days. In the next segment, there was a small wicker basket, woven with thin reeds in a fine weave. Inset in the lid was an ornate floral design of petit point. Caroline lifted the basket from the interior and examined it from all angles, then realized that she felt peculiar about opening it. Katherine Taggart was not some faceless phantom, an unknown figure from the past; she was the mistress of Katherine House and Jared's great-aunt. Though long dead, she survived so strongly in legend that to Caroline it was almost as if she were violating a friend's privacy by going through her things.

Repressing the voyeuristic feeling, Caroline lifted the lid. Inside were a satin pincushion with needles protruding, several bobbins of embroidery thread, a pair of embroidery scissors with ornate brass handles. And beneath the implements, a small wooden hoop over which was stretched a piece of white linen. As she lifted it out, the folds fell out of the linen, revealing it to be a square. A handkerchief. Small stitches drew a fleur-de-lis motif surrounding a monogram.

Caroline slanted the hoop toward the window to get a closer look at the half-finished initial in the center. Still threaded with pale blue floss, the needle had been anchored in the cloth, held there by a half-inch-wide swath of fabric, as though Katherine had put it aside temporarily, expecting to get back to it at any moment. Again Caroline experienced an odd sense of violating Katherine Taggart's privacy. She traced over the unfinished letter, a curved line that gracefully arched into the beginning of a downstroke—the crossbar of a capital *T*, for Taggart? Not likely, Caroline thought. The downstroke was too far left in the letter, not in the center. It looked more like a *C*. *C* for Colin? A gift for the beloved younger brother who adored her? Caroline had been on the way to her brother's college graduation when she was killed. Had she hoped to finish the handkerchief as a graduation gift? There was no way of knowing, but Caroline made a mental note to show it to Jared.

Thinking that the basket itself might make an interesting piece of bric-a-brac for some corner or shelf, Caroline replaced it in the well. As she did, her hand brushed a spiderweb, and she automatically recoiled, knocking over a small cut-crystal bottle. The glass stopper fell free, skittering across the floor of the storage well. Whatever had been in the bottle—perfume or cologne—had long since evaporated, but when the stopper dislodged, the essence of the scent wafted up. Lavender. It hung in the cross breeze, slightly cloying from age. Caroline righted the bottle and replaced the stopper, then closed the storage well. She sat down on the window seat, imagining Katherine Taggart sitting there, using the light from the windows to illumine her sewing as she made those tiny stitches.

Perfume in the window seat. In the days before air-conditioning and antiperspirants, Katherine Taggart must have dotted cologne on her wrists and behind her ears to feel fresh. Caroline was more intrigued than ever by the woman who'd come to this Victorian mansion as a teenage bride and left such a strong imprint of her personality that the house now bore her name. From all accounts she was beautiful, but Caroline had no idea what she looked like. She'd have to ask Jared if there were photographs of her.

Realizing that she was daydreaming, Caroline rose to continue her preliminary inventory of the window seats. When she lifted the time-dilapidated cushion on the next segment and tried to lift the lid, it refused to budge. Nor would the lid of the segment next to it. Caroline didn't think it was particularly significant that they had been sealed. None of the wells had been very full, so storage space was probably not at a major premium. But, curious, she knelt so that she was at eye level with the lids and looked for evidence of how they had been sealed.

She didn't have to look far, and what she found perplexed her. The lid was held down by a row of closely spaced nails along the outside edge. The crudity of the carpentry was in stark contrast to the quality workmanship evident else-where throughout the room. The carpenter had used nails with flat heads, an unusual choice, and the heads of the nails did not fit flush against the top of the lid, indicating that some of the nails had been driven in at an angle, instead of straight down. In one spot, the head of the hammer had left an indentation in the wood—a sign of inexperience, and sloppy even for an apprentice carpenter.

Categorizing the sealed lids and poor carpentry as one of those intriguing mysteries one runs into when renovating old houses—rather like a hidden passageway or cupboard—Caroline moved on to the seats that were open, and found additional memorabilia of daily life, interesting but not nearly so intimate as the sewing basket and cologne: a dog-eared copy of *Topper* by Thorne Smith and less worn copies of *Elmer Gantry* by Sinclair Lewis and *Scarlet Sister Mary* by Julia Peterkin, several issues of *The Saturday Evening Post* and *Ladies Home Journal* from 1929, a set of dominoes, a checkerboard and checkers. She was examining a pair of bridge decks in a teak box when she heard footsteps on the stairs.

"Caroline?" It was Jared's voice.

Caroline walked to the door and answered, "Up here."

"I've got a surprise for you."

"The Victrola!" she exclaimed, as he reached the second floor and moved into her view.

"All cleaned and oiled and ready to spin."

"It's beautiful," Caroline said, running her finger around the rim of the flower-horn speaker. "It looks brand-new."

"The man who serviced it said it was made in 1919—the year Katherine and Samuel were married. I remember my grandfather telling me that Katherine listened to it for hours on end. She'd always wanted one, but they were so poor—"

"So Samuel bought her one. That's sweet."

"If any of these records are playable, we can find out what kind of music she liked."

"Maybe there's music for the Charleston or the 'black bottom.'"

"With a husband in his fifties, and a town the size of Taggartville, I doubt if she had much opportunity to be a flapper." He lifted a record from the stack of twelve-inch discs and read, 'Ida, Sweet as Apple Cider.' 'Be Still, My Heart!'"

"That label looks newer than the rest," Caroline said, looking over his shoulder. "'Piccolo Pete,' by Ted Weems and His Orchestra. Have you ever heard of them?"

Jared shook his head. "Shall we listen?"

Caroline replied with a gasp of surprise. "What?" he asked.

"Al Jolson! 'Sonny Boy.' It looks brand-new."

"Jolson, I've heard of. Let's give a listen."

Caroline watched with interest as Jared cranked the phonograph and swiveled the stylus to position the needle on the record. The quality, compared to compact disc, was scratchy, but Jolson's talent was timeless; his voice charmed them through the scratches of primitive sound technology and more than half a century.

So did Weems and "Piccolo Pete," and Red Nichols and His Five Pennies with "Ida," and Ben Selvin with "Dardanella."

"It's like a time machine," Caroline said. "I can almost *feel* your great-aunt here, tapping her toe in time with the music." She looked up at Jared. "Do you think Taggart sat in here with her, listening with her, while she did her needlework?"

Jared smiled at her warmly. "If she was as pretty as you are, he'd have been crazy not to."

"The music must be getting to you," she said, smiling back. "You're waxing poetic."

It's not the music, Jared thought. He'd been captivated by her since the moment he spied her at the top of the stairs, dressed in shorts and an oversize jersey. A Harvard jersey. Even when she dressed down, she did it with a touch of class—that Boston polish. Her hair was loose, restrained only by a simple bandeau that held it back, away from her face. She looked young, desirable, delectable. "You keep smiling at me that way, and I might progress from slightly poetic to downright romantic," he warned.

He was close to crossing the line between light banter and serious flirting, and Caroline found she was responding more as a woman being flirted with than a co-worker engaged in light banter. She decided that ignoring his comments would be the best avenue of defense against her vulnerability to his charm. She didn't want to encourage him, but she didn't want to overreact to his teasing, either. He hadn't exactly patted her on the tush or made a grab for her; calling her pretty and admiring her smile hardly qualified as sexual harassment—

especially from someone as gregarious as Jared. Doling out outrageous compliments probably came as naturally to him as saying hello when he picked up a telephone. *And about as meaningful to him*, she reminded herself.

To distance herself from him she walked over to the window seat for the sewing basket. "I found something you might find interesting."

"Did you put some room deodorizer up here?" Jared asked, sniffing the air.

"Room deodorizer?" Caroline echoed.

"I smell . . . flowers or something."

"Oh," Caroline said, laughing softly. "That's very old lavender cologne. Katherine kept a bottle in the window seat."

She placed the basket in Jared's hands. "Your great-aunt's sewing basket. And look—" She removed the lid and lifted out the handkerchief, pointing to the unfinished initial. "This looks like the beginning of a C. I wondered if she was making it for your grandfather."

Jared lifted his shoulders. "He always kept a handkerchief in his pocket, but he never mentioned Katherine making any for him. There's probably no way we'll ever find out."

"I found something else," she said, and lifted her eyebrows dramatically. "A mystery." She showed him the sealed window seats and the row of nails.

He studied the nailheads curiously, and gave her a this-is-weird scowl.

"Any rumors of missing family treasures?" she asked lightly.

"None that I've ever heard." Still curious, he knelt and knocked on the front wall of the sealed seats with his fist. The resultant sound was a hollow thud. He knocked on the seat that held the afghan: same hollow thud. "If anything's in there, it can't be too bulky."

He straightened and brushed the dust from his knee. "For all we know, she may have given my grandfather a hammer and nails for Christmas and let him nail it shut so he could practice. One thing's for sure—we'll never know if there's anything in there unless we want to do extensive repairs afterward, and I don't think idle curiosity's worth the hassle."

The song on the Victrola was finished, and a scratching sound came through the flower horn. Jared lifted the needle and removed the disc, then picked up the next one in the stack they'd selected. "'Three O'Clock in the Morning.' Sounds romantic."

The song was lilting and sentimental, a waltz. "Dance music," Caroline decided aloud.

Jared held up his arms in invitation. "Would you do me the honor, m'dear?"

His guileless charm was irresistible. Caroline stepped into his arms, placing her right hand in his left and her left hand over his shoulder. His right hand settled on her waist, warm against the soft cotton of the jersey. They moved in circles through the beams of colored light cast by the stained-glass dome.

When Caroline missed a step and bumped into Jared or stepped on his toe, they both laughed. "Do you suppose Katherine and Samuel clowned around this way?" Caroline asked.

"You're fascinated by my great-aunt, aren't you?"

"I've seen inside her life. I feel as if I know her. Did you know she was my age when she died? I figured it out."

Jared's hold on her tightened perceptibly. "Young and beautiful . . . No one who knew her ever got over it."

"What did she look like?"

Jared pulled Caroline closer, slipping his hand around her waist to caress the small of her back. He said her name firmly, and his voice had a husky quality.

Caroline tilted her head back to look at his face questioningly. The answers she found in his eyes were explicit. The heated expression in their depths told her they were beyond discussion of his great-aunt, beyond frivolous role-playing and speculation over whether Katherine and old Samuel Taggart ever danced to the same music. This was private; it was real; it was Jared Colin dancing with Caroline Naylor, holding her in his arms, gazing at her longingly, desiring her.

Caroline didn't want to see that look there, that desire. It complicated everything: her job, their sharing the house. It put her heart in jeopardy. She didn't want to fall in love with Jared Colin. Jared—spoiled, rich, handsome Jared, who needed a proper political wife, but who didn't want a wife at all. She didn't want to fall in love and have to say goodbye in a few weeks. She didn't need a seat on that particular roller coaster when she was already trying to decide whether to leave Urbane!, and if so, whether to go to a larger firm or start her own business.

She didn't *need* the complication of becoming emotionally involved with Jared Colin; yet, when she looked into the desire in his eyes, she felt an answering warmth deep inside her. Knowing that she should pull away, put distance between them, she moved closer to him, enjoying the feel of a strong arm around her. She rested her cheek on his chest and sighed, enjoying the feel of his hard body against her breasts.

"You use shaving soap," she said.

"My beard's too heavy for an electric razor."

"It's the same soap my grandfather used," she said, thinking it an odd choice for him; she'd have thought he'd choose something more contemporary—a designer scent.

"My grandfather, too," he said.

The trace of sentimentality in his voice endeared him to her. His genuine fondness for his grandfather was obvious.

The Victrola was losing its crank; the music slowed, but Jared kept dancing. He'd been waiting to hold Caroline in his arms since the first time he saw her, and he was loath to let go of her. She felt too good nestled there—soft, warm, female. Her hair was velvet against his chin, smelling like exotic flowers.

She stopped dancing abruptly, and lifted her head to look at him. "The music stopped."

"Not for us," he said, and he lowered his mouth to hers.

6

CAROLINE HELD HER BREATH as she waited for the kiss. She was too susceptible to Jared's virility, too swept up in the romance of dancing to old records in the Kaleidoscope Room, for this waltz to end any other way.

He was gentle at first, as she knew he would be. Fantasy fused with reality as his lips brushed over hers lightly, testing, then returned for a leisurely nibble, an explorative taste. His right hand warmed the small of her back as he hugged her close. The fingers of his left hand combed through her hair to cradle her head. She was aware of everywhere he touched her—his chest solid against her more pliant breasts, his thighs hard against her bare thighs through the slightly nubby texture of his slacks. Her body tautened, then relaxed, melding acquiescently against his; her lips softened, opened.

Heartened by her response, Jared deepened the kiss with deliberate slowness. He'd waited too long to kiss her to hurry; he wanted to savor the experience. And savor it he did—the way her mouth conformed to his, the smoothness of her flesh as his tongue swept across her lower lip, the way she seemed to melt into his embrace, touching him in all the right places, affirming the elemental, complementary differences between them.

Purposefully, he kept the kiss chaste, knowing that if he took it too far she'd draw away from him: knowing that if he touched her breasts, or spread his hands over those delectable swells of buttocks and pulled her against his hardness, he wouldn't want to stop. Grudgingly accepting that the timing was wrong for anything more.

Caroline felt his slow withdrawal, the slackening of pressure of his mouth, the gradual loosening of his arm around her waist, the slide of his hand from her hair down to her cheek. She was glad he hadn't pressed for more, that there had been no frenzied groping, no insulting grab. There was only the mutual enjoyment of a kiss, which somehow fit the romance of the setting.

His hand was cradling her cheek as carefully as he might a fragile piece of glass. The expression of adoration in the depths of his eyes as he looked down at her face held her own gaze captive. Speechless, she looked up into those gorgeous blue eyes, feeling as though her bones might turn to jelly under their spell.

A warm tenderness toward him swelled in her chest, and she realized she'd fallen a bit in love with him. She had enough presence of mind to hope that it was a temporary aberration, a reaction to the moment. But then, with his fingertips still lightly caressing her face and his eyes reflecting the magic of the moment, he did something that proved to her that it was not temporary aberration or temporary madness: He smiled.

Caroline's breath lodged in her throat. God, but he was beautiful—and beautifully male. Those blue eyes, those cheekbones, that fair skin, the shadow of his dark beard. Those even teeth, full lips, that straight nose. His smile was hot enough to melt glaciers. Caroline felt it melting her resistance to the idea of loving him. She could imagine it on campaign posters, seducing the female vote.

That image brought her crashing back to reality, or at least, to enough of the reality for her to remember why she shouldn't be even the tiniest bit in love with Jared Colin. Her arms were still around his neck. Slowly she drew them away, letting her hands linger on his shoulders momentarily before dropping them to her sides.

Jared dropped his hands, too, and shoved them into his pockets in a gesture that was becoming familiar to Caroline. She searched for something to say to defuse the sudden awkwardness, but nothing came to mind. Jared appeared just as much at a loss for words until, abruptly, he took his hands from his pockets, placed one on each side of her face and bent to drop a fleeting kiss on her cheek on his way past her to the Victrola.

He picked up the small paper bag he'd carried in with the Victrola. "I almost forgot about this. It's a surprise for that screaming fur-ball with the highfalutin' name."

She smiled. "You bought Dessie a present?"

"I understood she gave away her favorite toy recently."

"Only temporarily."

"Where is she, anyway?"

"She was still hiding in my room the last time I checked. She doesn't like the stairs. I think they confuse her."

"I don't know much about cats," Jared said, as Caroline reached into the bag. "They're supposed to like catnip, aren't they?"

"Some do, some don't. Dessie goes nutso over it." The new toy was a plastic bubble filled with catnip and suspended on a springy base that attached to the floor with a suction cup. She held the base in her left hand and thumped the plastic bubble with the thumb and forefinger of her right. It bobbled jauntily. "She's going to love batting this around."

"I thought it made more sense than something that would roll around and fall down the stairs."

"Good thinking," Caroline agreed. "Would you like to give it to her? I can try to flush her out—"

"No sense in doing that. It might just upset her more."

"I'll wait until she's in a friendly mood," Caroline said, then winked. "I'll be sure to tell her who it's from."

Jared glanced at his watch. "I didn't realize how late it was. I've got a meeting at seven." A chamber of commerce steering-committee meeting. It was going to be boring as hell, but he *had* to become a part of the community, and serving on the committee no one else wanted to serve on seemed like an expedient way.

He cocked an eyebrow. "Want to grab a quick dinner?"

The thought of going out in public made Caroline suddenly aware of how grubby she was from rummaging around in the Kaleidoscope Room all afternoon. She looked down at her dusty jersey and then up at Jared. "I don't think so. I've got a date."

Jared's eyes narrowed. A date? She'd been in town two days, and she had a date? He might have known he'd have competition for a woman as attractive as Caroline Naylor.

"With a pizza, your great-aunt's diary and that claw-footed bathtub in my suite!" she said, although why she felt obligated to clarify that she didn't have a date with a man, she didn't know. Maybe it was because he'd just kissed her.

No, she decided. *It wasn't because he'd kissed her. It was because she'd kissed him back!*

He raised his hand to run his fingers through her hair and cradle her head, forcing her to look at him. Her shocked gaze met his, only to find raw desire burning in the deep blue depths of his eyes. While she was still frozen with surprise, he lowered his mouth to hers for a kiss—brief, but fierce in its intensity.

He broke off the kiss as abruptly as he'd launched into it. The expression in his eyes was even more volatile than before. He pulled his hand from her hair and flicked her nose with his forefinger. "Think of me when you're wet and slippery, Sugar Lips."

Caroline watched in mute consternation as he walked away. *Sugar Lips!* He was teasing, he had to be. He couldn't possibly be serious. "I ought to slap your face for that!" she said, just as he reached the door.

He turned and gave her an infuriatingly cocky grin. "Just trying to indulge the fantasy of a lonely woman, Sugar Lips. Next time we dance I'll bring wine—unless you'd prefer beer."

He was gone before she could come up with a sufficiently vile retort, his footsteps echoing in the old house as he descended the stairs. Sugar Lips! Why had she ever goaded him with that stupid comment about construction workers? "It'll be a cold day in hell before you ever see my twin peaks," she muttered.

Fuming, she decided to call it a day. She still had unpacking to do, and after finding the sewing basket and listening to Katherine's records, she was more anxious than ever to start reading Katherine Taggart's diary. Still holding Desdemona's new toy, she gave the Kaleidoscope Room one final look-over and then went downstairs to her own room.

She called Desdemona, fixed the suction cup to the floor and flipped the toy a few times. Desdemona sniffed at the plastic bubble curiously, then gave it a few swipes of her tongue trying to get at the catnip before deciding, apparently, that it wasn't worth her attention. With a haughty look and a meow, she sauntered out of the room, crooked tail held high.

"I'm going to tell Jared you said that!" Caroline retorted, then went into the bathroom to draw her bath, adding a few drops of her favorite bath oil. "One of us has to have some backbone where he's concerned."

After some consideration of the matter, she decided that reading the diary in the tub was too perilous, and opted for the "Florida's Young Stallions" magazine article instead.

They met at the Florida State University. Young men of privilege and potential, they belonged to the most prestigious fraternity, drove the hottest cars and dated the prettiest coeds.

I'll bet! Caroline thought wryly, then read on.

Three of them routinely made the dean's list. They were, from their beginning college years, trendsetters rather than followers, known for their innovations in fashion and for their creative high-jinks. One shocked the campus Greek community by showing up at the annual formal gala in a tuxedo jacket and tropical-print surf shorts. Another convinced the Seminole Boosters Club president to serve fried alligator-tail meat at a luncheon preceding the FSU-UF football game.

They became known, early in their college careers, as The Stallions, reminiscent of the BMOC—Big Men on Campus—of the sixties. They became Florida State University's equivalent to Hollywood's Brat Pack, and it was commonly accepted that by the tenth anniversary of their graduation year, each would either be famous or dead. But even the most stalwart Stallion watchers have been amazed by the marks these Young Stallions have made in their respective fields scarcely five years after graduation.

Caroline skimmed most of the rest of the article, but paid close attention to the sections about Jared, which included a thumbnail sketch of his background that identified him as heir to the Colin's Breads fortune and grandson of former governor Mitchell Colin.

She read about his jet-black hair, his "blue eyes that always seem to have the twinkle of mischief," his distinctive style of dress that "created the impression that he'd shopped for his clothes at a shop run by a schizophrenic fashion designer."

"That's Jared, all right!" she mumbled to the bathroom walls.

And then she thought: *Sugar Lips!*

And then she giggled, because she realized that she was wet and slippery and thinking about Jared.

And that's when she put the magazine article aside, slid down into the water until her neck was cradled on the rounded rim of the tub and remembered how it felt to be kissed by Jared Colin.

The warm water, fragrant from the bath oil, was lulling. Gradually it leeched the tension of her whirlwind travel preparations, the long drive and the excitement of visiting Taggartville and Katherine House from her body. She relaxed—really relaxed—for the first time since Jared called her office wanting her to oversee the restoration. Her breathing slowed and deepened. Her eyes drifted shut.

She was half a dream away from a kiss when she was rudely awakened by a loud thrumming. For a few seconds she sat at attention in the now tepid water trying, in a state of near sleep, to put the strange noise in perspective. It was coming from the next room. It was too irregular to be mechanical.

Caroline slid back down into the tub on a sigh of relief, as she realized it was Desdemona, swatting at her new toy. Thank you very much for scaring the living daylights out of me, Mr. Jared Colin. She pried the stopper out of the drain with her big toe and air dried as the water slowly seeped from the tub.

Refreshed, she put on a set of lightweight sweats and called out for pizza. Then she snuggled up in bed with Katherine Taggart's diaries to wait for the deliveryman. She ate in her room instead of the kitchen, then carried the leftovers to the kitchen before going back to the diaries.

Katherine Taggart was not the most creative writer in history, but her day-to-day account of life made interesting reading because of the attitudes and perspectives revealed in her journal entries, and her reactions to news events of the day. The earliest entry was in 1926. Caroline could see potential in publishing selected excerpts that mentioned news events of the time—the hurricane of 1926, and so on. She made a mental note to pick up some colored paper flags at the office supply so she could mark some of the more intriguing passages as she read.

Whether it was Katherine Taggart's prose or the enervating effects of the bath, she dozed off sometime between the September hurricane and Halloween of 1926.

It wasn't Desdemona playing with her new toy that awakened her this time, it was Desdemona's howling. Caroline opened her eyes just soon enough to see the cat almost kill herself in a mad dash across the wood floors to get under the bed. Caroline leaned over the edge and saw her crouched there, growling deep in her throat.

"No more catnip for you!" she said. "I don't know what's gotten into you." And then she heard it, too.

"Criminy, Dessie, it's only music." *But not just any music. "Three O'Clock in the Morning." The song she and Jared had danced to. On the Victrola.* Caroline couldn't blame Dessie for being skittish. As the music filtered down from the Kaleidoscope Room the whole ceiling seemed to reverberate with it. Dessie wasn't accustomed to noise coming from on high!

Involuntarily Caroline smiled. She might have known Jared would be at the bottom of the mayhem. She really must have been zonked not to hear him enter the house and walk up the stairs.

The music faded, then began again at the beginning. Caroline dragged out of bed and went to the bathroom to brush her hair and her teeth and put on lipstick. "You could have just knocked at my door," she grumbled, looking up at the ceiling. "But no, not Jared Colin. Jared Colin has to do everything on a grand scale!"

Satisfied with her reflection, she shrugged her shoulders and headed for the stairs, wondering whether Jared had brought wine or beer.

Both, she decided. Jared wouldn't do anything halfway!

The door to the Kaleidoscope Room was closed. Typically, Jared was going to milk the scene for all it was worth. She reached the landing and raised her hand to knock, but held her fist suspended in the air when she heard a voice inside the room. Jared, talking to himself?

If he was, then he answered himself—in a damned convincing falsetto that was followed by a peal of laughter that bore no resemblance to Jared's hearty belly-laugh. Caroline snatched her hand back as though the door might grow teeth and devour it at any second.

Her cheeks burned with humiliation as she tiptoed back down the stairs, appalled at how close she'd come to making a complete fool of herself. She didn't comprehend just how big a fool she would have been to knock on that door until she reached her room and heard the footfalls on the floor above. Rhythmic footfalls that tamped out the waltz beat of the music. Dancing. Accompanied by muffled voices, male and female, with intermittent high-pitched laughter.

Caroline tried to be reasonable. It was his house, his Victrola, his business. She had no claim on him, no right to be offended. Except that he'd danced with her in that very room not eight hours earlier. Not even six, she amended, looking at the clock. He'd danced with her to that very song and laughed with her when they missed a step and then he'd kissed her.

He'd kissed her, and she'd gotten all gushy inside like a girl who'd been to her first dance. Caroline grabbed a pillow from the bed and punched it with all her might. Maybe she had no claim on Jared, but his lack of sensitivity was unforgivable. He must know she could hear the music, the dancing, the laughter. Could he be so blasé as to think she wouldn't be offended?

She punched the pillow again. *Damn him! He'd promised to bring wine!*

The music faded into silence, but the dancing continued for almost a minute.

"*The music stopped.*"

"*Not for us.*"

The memory replayed in Caroline's mind, setting off remembered emotions she'd rather have forgotten under the circumstances. When the gliding footsteps ceased, she closed her eyes, wishing she could escape the image of Jared above her, repeating the same lines to another gullible woman, kissing her. *Calling her Sugar Lips?*

Damn it! It shouldn't matter so much. She should be glad he was being a total jackass, relieved that she was lucky enough to find out about Jared Colin before she *really* got involved with him. She stood up straight, consciously stiffening her spine. She wasn't hurt; she refused to be hurt. She was too *furious* to be hurt by his callous insensitivity. She flopped down onto the bed, hugging the pillow to her chest. She was *not* going to let Jared Colin get to her again with his hokey charm and his little-boy grin and his lady-killer smile and his blue eyes with the twinkle of mischief and his bizarre, schizophrenic designer wardrobe.

That was when the new noises started above. Intimate noises. Heavy breathing and sighs and low, sexy moans. Noises no decent person would expect to hear except in a seedy XXX-rated movie house. Caroline put the pillow aside and sat up, trying to decide what to do. Homicide came to mind, but she immediately ruled that out, since she didn't own a weapon.

More's the pity, she thought, then sighed. *Get a grip on yourself, Caroline! You're not a violent person. You don't want to kill him.*

Right. Not when the possibility of sneaking downstairs in the middle of the night and tying him up and torturing him was so appealing.

Homicide? Torture? You're freaking out!

"Well, I'm not going to sit here and be subjected to this embarrassing concert of passion and mindless sex," she said aloud, half hoping that her voice would filter through the ceiling, but knowing the couple upstairs was beyond noticing if it did.

"Well, I've got something you *will* hear!" she said, and opened the carrying case in which she stored her music cassettes. Finding the tape she was looking for, she popped it into her boom box. "You like making whoopee?" she muttered. "Want some fireworks? Here's the Fourth of July, just for you!" She flicked on the tape player and turned the volume up as high as it would go.

Even a pillow over each ear couldn't down out the marches of John Philip Sousa played at full volume. Beneath her, the bed vibrated with Dessie's low growls.

It seemed an eternity before the tape ended and the machine switched itself off. Caroline tentatively let the pillows fall away from her ears, afraid of hearing even more embarrassing noises from upstairs. But there was only silence. Even Desdemona had stopped her growling.

The old house was still. Eerily so.

7

CAROLINE FROWNED WHEN SHE spied Jared's car in his usual parking space. She'd managed to get out of the house without running into him, and she'd hoped that he'd be gone by the time she returned from her shopping. Gathering bags from the discount store and supermarket, she carried them in the back door, hoping to get in and out of the kitchen and up the stairs without encountering him. She was still embarrassed and furious every time she thought of the evening before—embarrassed because she'd let herself get caught up in the romance of the moment and succumbed to his seductive charms, and furious over his lack of common decency.

She tiptoed in, closing the door behind her as quietly as possible, but Jared must have heard her, because he was in the kitchen by the time she'd put her frozen foods away.

"Good morning," he said with enough cheer to make her want to lob the head of lettuce in her hand at him.

"For some people, I suppose."

"Been doing some shopping."

"A person has to eat."

"You're much too pretty to be this grumpy in the morning."

"I can be as grumpy as I damned well please." Caroline slammed the refrigerator door. She refused to look at him as she stalked out of the room, fearful that if she saw his cajoling grin she'd be tempted to do or say something unladylike.

Jared followed her out of the kitchen, through the dining room and into the Grand Salon, but she didn't look back.

"Tell me, Ms. Naylor, did you get too close to that freezer just now, or did you overdose on Sousa last night?"

Caroline paused on the second step to glare at him. "Don't you *dare* talk to me about Sousa!"

He threw up his hands and shrugged, feigning innocence. "Whatever you say, Sugar Lips."

Her voice lowered an octave. "And don't *ever* call me Sugar Lips again!"

He clicked his heels together. *"Jawohl!"*

Caroline was relieved that he hadn't followed her up the stairs. Maybe he'd gotten the message. Still, she tensed when she heard him call out, "I gave you credit for a sense of humor!"

She almost dashed down the stairs to strangle him. A sense of humor? *A sense of humor!* Of all the unmitigated gall, the egotistical arrogance, the sheer nerve. A sense of humor? She surveyed the room, the wide hallway, and then looked into the room clogged with furniture and miscellaneous junk. There had to be something she could throw at him. An old iron, perhaps. An anvil. A machete.

Sucking in a deep breath for composure, she carried the rest of her purchases into her room and tossed them on the bed. If she hadn't come so far, and if she weren't so enchanted by the idea of working in Katherine House, she'd pack up and leave without so much as a fare-thee-well or a backward glance. But the contract was signed, and she was hooked on Katherine House. She was just going to have to act like an adult and keep her dealings with Jared on a professional level. And she would—as soon as she could look at him again without wanting to scratch his eyes out! In the interim, she was simply going to avoid him. She had enough work to keep her busy for days, possibly weeks, without having to consult with Mr. Jared Colin, or run anything by him for approval. He'd hired her to do a job, and by golly, she'd do it—without making the mistake of falling victim to his smarmy charm again.

She didn't have to worry about today, anyway. She had a morning meeting with members of the Taggartville Historical Preservation Society at Aunt Essie's, and afterward, Aunt Essie was taking her on a guided tour of the area's antique shops.

Caroline knew that by the time they'd exhausted the antique stores, she'd be ready for a quiet dinner at some out-of-the way restaurant, followed by another soak in the claw-footed tub and a couple of hours of reading Katherine Taggart's journals to unwind. Then, if Jared had enough sense not to bring a woman friend home for a tryst in the Kaleidoscope Room, she might even get a good night's sleep.

She was freshening up before leaving for Aunt Essie's when she heard the thrumming of Desdemona's new toy, and walked into the other room to observe. Desdemona swatted the plastic bubble with her paw, drew back as the toy vibrated on the spring, moving her head from side to side as she watched it bounce back and forth.

"Traitor!" Caroline accused. "You *would* like it."

Dessie gave it another whack. "Go right ahead," Caroline said. "Pretend it's Jared's head. In fact, you can pretend it's any choice part of his anatomy, and give it a few swipes for me!"

JARED'S CAR WAS GONE when Caroline returned to Katherine House just after eight that evening. She heaved a sigh of relief. If trooping from store to store meeting shop owners and taking notes didn't provide justification for a whopping headache, listening to Aunt Essie extol the virtues of Jared Colin for hours on end certainly did. Caroline had been prepared for a running commentary on Essie's children and grandchildren and her growing number of great-grandchildren, but the hard sell on Jared Colin had come as a total surprise.

Jared was smart. Jared was rich. Jared was civic-minded. Jared was *so* nice. And *so* nice looking. He was Governor Colin's grandson, a fact that, in itself, seemed to qualify him for canonization in Aunt Essie's book. It had taken Caroline all of a minute and a half in Aunt Essie's company to realize that she viewed Jared's bachelorhood as a sacred challenge and was bound and determined to save him from his solitary existence.

"It's just not natural for a man to live alone," she'd said. "He's not one of those . . . funny ones, you know. Of course, you *know*. You're a decorator."

Caroline was glad Aunt Essie was wound up enough not to require responses to any of her comments as she continued, "No, sir. That Jared Colin is all man."

Receiving no encouragement from Caroline, Aunt Essie steamed on. "I wouldn't be surprised if that boy went into politics. He's Governor Colin's grandson, you know."

"Yes," Caroline murmured. "I heard that somewhere." She'd heard it at least half a dozen times from Aunt Essie's lips on this very day!

"He's going to be quite a catch for some lucky girl."

And it had been quite obvious which lucky girl Aunt Essie had in mind. Caroline had thought it odd that Aunt Essie had condoned her living in Katherine House. Now she knew why, and her head ached with the strain of feigning total obliviousness to Aunt Essie's blatant matchmaking attempts.

She took two headache tablets and a hot bath. If she hadn't been afraid she'd run into Jared, she would have gone downstairs to watch television for a while. Instead, having nothing better to do, she crawled into bed with Katherine's journals, glad, at least, that she had been spared any new confrontations with Jared after her emotionally draining day.

DESDEMONA WOKE CAROLINE up at exactly two thirty-eight. Caroline knew it was two thirty-eight because she opened one eye to consult the lighted dial of her alarm clock. She closed her eye again and groaned. Dessie mewed and nudged Caroline's hands with her nose.

"Dessie?" Caroline murmured groggily. "What is *wrong* with you?"

Dessie climbed on Caroline's chest and mewed urgently, then jumped back onto the bedspread and restlessly paced the length of Caroline's body, nudging her every few inches.

Caroline groaned again and pushed up, bracing herself on her elbows. "Just see if I ever take you on a trip again!"

Desdemona leaped to the floor, then looked back at Caroline and mewed.

"All right, all right!" Caroline said, sitting up and dropping her feet over the edge of the bed. "This had better be something more urgent than an empty food dish. It was full when I went to bed."

She turned on the bedside lamp, then followed Desdemona to the center of the room. Desdemona stopped, mewed and circled Caroline's ankles twice. "Dessie, two thirty-eight in the morning is no time for ring-around-the-rosy."

As though she'd understood, Dessie set off again, pausing after a few steps to make sure Caroline was following before proceeding into the bathroom.

Caroline turned on the overhead light on her way inside. "I don't know what's gotten into—" But suddenly she *did* know what had Dessie so upset, because Dessie showed her, proudly.

Caroline did what any red-blooded young woman would do when presented with a dead mouse—a bloodied dead mouse—by her cat at two thirty-eight in the morning: She screamed. At the top of her lungs.

By the time Jared banged on the door, she had regained enough presence of mind to put on her chenille housecoat, specifically bought for the boardinghouse situation she'd anticipated in Taggartville. It was feminine but sexless, a one-size-fits-all wrap style guaranteed to make any wearer appear utterly shapeless.

When riled, Jared proved to be a very impatient man. The entire house seemed to rattle as he banged on the door. "Caroline? Caroline! Open this door!"

He was shouting, and he sounded terrified, which gave Caroline a feeling of smug satisfaction. Personally, she was feeling quite calm. The scream had been very cathartic.

"I'm going to break the door down, Caroline. Don't panic."

She opened it to save him the trouble, catching him in the middle of what might eventually have grown into a karate maneuver. Caroline didn't know much about karate, but she guessed that if, in fact, that was what Jared was attempting, he'd learned it from watching old movies rather than in a classroom.

He dropped his foot to the floor and heaved a sigh of relief. "Thank God you're all right."

"It's nice to know you care," she said letting saccharine sweetness ooze through her forced smile.

He waited for an explanation. He waited in vain. "You scared the hell out of me!" he said at last, making it sound like an accusation.

"Sorry," she said. "I'll try not to do it again. I wouldn't want to stunt your growth or anything."

"All right, Caroline, what's going on?" He looked as indignant as a man could look while wearing nothing but a pair of soft cotton drawstring pajama bottoms that rode about an inch below his waist.

Caroline noted, begrudgingly, that nothing about his growth appeared to have been stunted by anything, ever. His chest was perfect, his stomach was flat and hard, his biceps beautifully developed, his belly button cute. Even his feet were nice—long and slim, with high arches.

"Well?" he prompted.

"Desdemona."

"What about Desdemona?"

"She appreciated your gesture of generosity so much that she decided to reciprocate." She stalked to the bathroom, knowing he would follow. Stopping about three feet from the corpse, she spread out her arm toward it. "It's all yours, landlord."

Jared looked at the mouse, at Caroline, at the mouse, at Caroline. "What the hell am I supposed to do with a dead mouse?"

"Get rid of it."

"How?"

Caroline planted her hands on her waist impatiently. Men were undoubtedly the most helpless creatures on earth. "You could call the county coroner," she suggested blithely.

Jared scowled furiously. "What do you want me to do?"

"You don't expect *me* to touch it!" she said incredulously. "Dead mice aren't in my contract."

"Oh, all right," he growled, and then muttered, "Women! They're damned liberated—until you put a mouse in front of them."

"It's your house, and it's your mouse."

"It's your cat."

"Don't worry—there's no extra charge for extermination services."

They glared at each other for a moment. Jared frowned. "Did I see you with a plastic shopping bag this morning?"

Caroline nodded. "It's in the trash basket."

Jared fished it out and slipped it over his hand. He picked up the mouse, reversed the bag back over his hand, and over the mouse. Then, when he flipped his hand over, the mouse was securely inside the bag. He twisted the top of the bag closed, then tied it in a knot before dropping the whole bundle in the trash can with a thump.

"It was dirty, dangerous work," he said, leveling his gaze on Caroline's face. "But somebody had to do it."

"Wash your hands," Caroline said, avoiding looking at him, trying not to remember the play of muscles on his back as he'd bent over and scooped up the mouse.

"Yes, mom," Jared said, stepping up to the sink.

Caroline balled up a strip of toilet tissue and wiped the blood off the floor where the mouse had been, tossed it into the toilet and flushed it, then waited for Jared to move away from the sink so she could wash her hands, too.

She fought not to look at Jared, not to stare at that broad expanse of hair-sprinkled flesh. She hadn't even realized she'd lost the battle until Jared flicked water from his hand to his chest and grinned lasciviously. "What do you say, Sugar Lips. Wanta pretend it's sweat?"

"Get out!" She stalked past him into the bedroom, which, ironically, seemed less intimate than the bathroom because of its size. She stood in the middle of the room with her back to the bathroom door, unconsciously clutching at the lapels of her chenille robe.

"It doesn't work, you know."

"What?" she asked, without turning around.

"Hiding in that fuzzy robe. You're still sexy. And I'd be willing to bet you've got on something very sexy underneath all that fuzz."

"What I have on under this fuzz is none of your business."

A tense silence followed. Finally Caroline said, "I asked you to leave."

"You ordered me to get out."

"Good for me."

Another silence ensued. "Why don't you tell me what you're so hopping mad about."

Caroline turned to face him defiantly, jutting her chin. "You're not stupid."

"No! And I'm not clairvoyant, either. This isn't just over my calling you Sugar Lips, is it?"

"Give me a little credit, would you?"

"How about giving me a break? At least tell me why you're suddenly blowing arctic air in my direction."

Caroline elevated her chin half an inch. "You can drop the innocent act. It isn't working."

A sound came from Jared's throat that could have been correctly described as a growl. "One of us is two bricks shy of a load, and it isn't me."

"Two bricks shy of a load," she repeated sarcastically. "Isn't that quaint. You do 'real people' so well. An expression like that ought to be good for hundreds of votes."

Jared drove his fingers into his hair in a gesture of despair. "Damn it, Caroline. At least tell me why you've done a complete about-face."

"As if you didn't know."

Jared capped her shoulders with his hands and shoved his face near hers. "You kissed me yesterday!"

"That was a mistake."

Some of the anger drained from his expression. "It didn't feel like a mistake to me."

He was too close. The gleam in his eye as he looked down at her face was too seductive. Caroline didn't like the effect he was having on her senses. She shrugged her shoulders free and turned away. A long silence followed. Although she couldn't see him and he wasn't touching her, Caroline was aware of Jared's presence and proximity, of the intimacy of his bare chest and feet, of those low-slung drawstring pajama bottoms.

"Is there someone else?" he asked with devastating tenderness. Caroline stiffened her spine, but didn't answer. "If there is, tell me. I'll understand. We can be friends."

She spun to face him. "I'm not quite as understanding."

He appeared genuinely perplexed, which perplexed Caroline.

"What?" he said finally, exhaling the word in a weary sigh. "Me? You think I'm involved with someone else?"

Her eyes narrowed. "I may be gullible, Jared, but I'm not deaf—or stupid."

Shaking his head in disbelief, he threw up his hands. "I give up!"

"Does this mean you'll leave?"

"I might as well. I can't defend myself if I don't know what it is I'm supposed to have done."

"I heard it all," she said with the deadly calm of contained rage. "The music, the laughing, the dancing, the—" She swallowed, remembering the groans of passion. "Everything!"

Jared emitted an exasperated groan. "Would you *please* tell me what you're talking about?"

"Oh, give it up, Jared! You had a woman up there, and it was obvious what was going on."

"What woman? Up where?"

"In the Kaleidoscope Room, of course. Last night." Jared might have argued, but she didn't give him a chance. "I don't give a damn what you do or with whom, but I'd appreciate it if you'd have enough common decency not to do it within my hearing." *Especially when it's an instant replay of the scene you'd shared with me a few hours before.* "This may be your house, but this suite is my home while I'm working here, and I have a right not to be subjected to your . . . *carnal escapades.*"

Jared was looking at her as though she'd lost her mind. "Honey, I'd love to confess and say I'm sorry, but I haven't had any carnal escapades within recent memory."

"How can you stand there and deny it after mentioning the Sousa this morning?"

Jared was speechless a moment, then said, "The Sousa you were playing last night?"

Caroline scowled at him.

"I want to get this straight," he said. "The Sousa music had something to do with my carnal escapades?"

"Why do you think I was playing John Philip Sousa loud enough to wake the dead? I heard what was going on upstairs, and I was trying to let you know, without the humiliation of *interrupting* you, that you weren't alone."

"I don't know what you heard, or what you think you heard, but I assure you, the closest experience I've ever had to a carnal escapade in this house was with you yesterday afternoon. And it didn't involve Sousa."

"So you're denying it?"

"Caroline, I was at the most boring committee meeting in the history of chambers of commercedom last night. I may have indulged in a few fantasies involving what might qualify as a carnal escapade, but I assure you I was nowhere near the Kaleidoscope Room, and fantasy is as close as I got to ecstasy. And when I got home, it sounded as though an entire brass band was marching through the house playing 'The Stars and Stripes Forever.'"

"Drowning out the embarrassing sounds from the Kaleidoscope Room."

"The sounds of a carnal escapade?"

"Don't you dare make fun of me!"

"Do you have a history of erotic hallucinations?"

"Hallucinations, my Aunt Hattie's hatpins!" she snapped, showing her irritation with a challenging, feet-apart stance. "You were up there with a woman, playing the Victrola—among other things. Maybe you didn't realize that sound travels down very easily, and that I'd hear you dancing and—commingling."

Jared chuckled. "Commingling?"

His amusement fueled Caroline's anger. "If you weren't here, how do you explain hearing the Sousa."

"I heard the Sousa when I came home from the committee meeting in the back room of the Cow Café."

"You could have the grace to be embarrassed, instead of pretending it never happened."

Jared's face reflected concern. "You're serious, aren't you?"

"As a tax audit."

He cupped her elbow and led her to one of the chairs next to the window-side table, then sat opposite her. "Maybe you'd better tell me exactly what you heard."

Comprehension dawned on her face. "*You're* serious, too."

"Caroline, I was with at least half a dozen people last night, if you'd care to talk to them."

"But if you weren't upstairs, then who—?"

"Who, indeed?"

Caroline frowned dubiously. "You expect me to believe that someone just came into your house, went up to the Kaleidoscope Room, played the Victrola and then had sex—without your knowledge or permission?"

"If you heard someone up there commingling in a carnal escapade, that's exactly what happened."

"If? Jared, I'm not an impressionable, sex-starved spinster with an overactive imagination. I don't have to rely on erotic hallucinations to get my jollies."

"No one's implying that."

"Aren't you? It's your phrase—'erotic hallucinations.'"

"I was teasing at the time. But I'm not teasing anymore. Someone was in the house last night, trespassing. From what you've told me, they mustn't have known you were here. You could have been in danger if you'd confronted them directly and they'd panicked."

Caroline considered that a moment. She'd come so close to knocking on the Kaleidoscope Room door. What if she hadn't heard the laughter, the female voice? If she'd surprised intruders— But no, it didn't make sense. "People don't just break into houses and decide to have sex."

"Burglars don't, no. But kids out for a thrill—" He shrugged his shoulders. "I'm not even sure the doors were locked, unless you locked them."

"I locked the front door after my pizza was delivered. I didn't do anything with the back door."

"I usually lock it when I leave, but it's an old lock. You could probably find a key that fits it in a junk shop."

Caroline hugged herself as reaction set in. If she had confronted prowlers, scared them—

"People have always been fascinated by Katherine House, especially the locals, who've heard all the legends. It was probably just curious kids with nothing better to do. They could have seen me leave and, not realizing you were here, decided to look around."

"And then decided to play the Victrola, dance, and make mad, passionate love?"

Jared grinned. "You're supposed to be the romantic. They found the Victrola, danced a little and got caught up in the romantic spell." His eyes swept over her face warmly. "It happens to people, you know. It happened to us."

Caroline leaped up. "Oh, my God!"

Jared rose, too. "Caroline?"

"The Victrola!" she said. "The records. They could have smashed up everything in the room and I wouldn't have heard them."

"Or carried them off," Jared pointed out. "You haven't been up there today?"

She shook her head.

"Then maybe we'd better take a look."

The scent of lavender wafted out of the Kaleidoscope Room as they opened the door. Moonlight floated through stained glass, giving the room an eery, twilight quality, like a stage illuminated with colored lights and swathed in gauze curtains. Caroline held her breath while Jared made his way to the floor lamp and flicked it on, then exhaled slowly in relief when she spied the Victrola, apparently unharmed.

Then it struck Caroline: the absolute sameness of the room. There was a strangeness, a peculiar familiarity about it that sent a shiver up her spine.

"Caroline?"

"I can't explain it," she whispered. "It was just . . . a feeling. It's as though it's *never* been touched. Not last night, not yesterday afternoon, not since Katherine Taggart was here." She forced a laugh. "That sounds crazy, doesn't it?"

"Nothing sounds crazy at this time of night. Obviously our intruders, whoever they were, were careful to leave everything just the way they found it."

"We were lucky, then."

"Yes. In more ways than one." He paused, deep in thought. "I'm going to have new locks installed."

"You can't deface the doors! They're original."

"Better the doors than my decorator," he said gravely. "There are bound to be locks specifically designed for old houses. We'll check it out. Tomorrow."

He glanced at the clock they'd wound the day before. It was still ticking, the second hand still moving. "Or rather, today. Right now, I think we ought to test the Victrola."

Caroline's mind was not as sharp as it could have been. "Test it?" she asked, stifling a yawn.

Jared smiled slyly. "It's exactly three o'clock in the morning."

Caroline comprehended, and returned his smile. "The name of the song."

Jared, who'd cranked the Victrola, waited for the turntable to build up to speed, and then put the stylus in place. Turning, he opened his arms to dance posture. "I'd say it's destiny, wouldn't you?"

"I don't call anything anything at three o'clock in the morning. But I don't argue much, either." She stepped into his arms and rested her cheek against his bare chest, snuggling when she discovered that the light covering of hair was softer than she'd anticipated. "Maybe it was ghosts," she murmured groggily. "Maybe we stirred up the shades of old Samuel and Katherine Taggart."

"I think I like you at three o'clock in the morning," Jared said, pulling her a little closer.

"You're not going to like me or Dessie much when your alarm goes off at seven."

"I'll worry about that at seven," he said, and kissed her temple.

8

"THANKS FOR DINNER," Caroline said. Her voice, slightly breathless from a lingering kiss, tickled over his senses like a feather on a soft breeze.

"How about dessert?" he asked, hearing the huskiness of sexual arousal in his voice.

"You've already had dessert!" she said firmly, easing away from him.

"It wasn't spumoni I had in mind." They'd been to Taggartville's only Italian restaurant.

"It's obvious what's on your mind."

"Good. Then I don't have to explain. I can just indulge." She acquiesced easily as he guided her back into his arms, and responded warmly as he kissed her. She was also the one who ended the kiss, pushing him away with a gentle shove and an equally gentle smile.

"You have a meeting, remember?"

"I'll skip it."

"And let the chamber of commerce down?" she asked lightly.

"To hell with the chamber of commerce."

He searched her face for encouragement, waiting for a whispered entreaty for him to forget the meeting and stay with her. He was trying not to rush her, but every time they kissed, patience became a bigger virtue.

All he found in her expression was reluctance over their parting, and her words were in the same light vein as before. "What kind of attitude is that for an aspiring grass-roots politician?"

A knot of disappointment settled in Jared's gut. His gaze locked with hers significantly. "There's more to life than politics."

She closed her eyes, shuttering herself away from the intensity of the desire she saw in the depths of his, and sighed. "Go to your meeting, Jared."

"I know. I'm going." He grinned mischievously and dropped a kiss on her nose on his way to the door. Before closing it behind him, though, he stuck his head back in the house and said, "But I'll be ba-a-a-ack!"

"Stick your head back in here again and I'll bean you with a frying pan," Caroline threatened.

Laughing, Jared closed the door but reopened it immediately. "Hold off on the frying pan!"

"What do you want now?"

You, Jared thought. *I want you.* But he said, "Don't forget to relock the doors if you open them for any reason."

"Who are you? The sheriff's home-security adviser?" Caroline asked.

"After last week—"

"I'll lock them, I promise. Now, get out of here before you're late for your meeting."

"Caroline?"

She looked at him exasperatedly.

"You're cute."

"And you're incorrigible," Caroline countered.

"It's just part of my charm, Sugar Lips."

Caroline stared at the door a few seconds after he'd gone. Unfortunately, he was right. Incorrigibility was a part of his charm. Jared Colin: spoiled rotten and naughty to the bone. Charming. Sexy. Outrageous. One of Florida's Young Stallions. And despite all her resolve to the contrary, every day she was near him she fell a little more in love with him.

It was folly, of course. She was headed for a broken heart. She was only going to be in Florida long enough to finish the

Katherine House project, and even if she were staying, she couldn't picture herself happy as an arm ornament for a pretty-boy political aspirant. The question was: Just how deeply did she want to get involved while she was here?

It was not a question with quick or simple answers; certainly not a dilemma that could be resolved by standing in the middle of the floor staring at the back door. She had work she could be doing upstairs.

Dessie was sitting in the second-floor hallway at the top of the stairs. Caroline sat down on the top step to pet her. "He is incorrigible you know," she told the cat, then frowned. "But, somehow, with Jared, it seems more like a genetic trait than a character flaw. Everything about the man is exasperating and endearing at the same time."

Dessie rubbed her head against Caroline's hip, then rolled on her back so Caroline could scratch her chest. She purred contentedly as Caroline obliged her.

Cats were so simply mollified, Caroline thought. If only men were as easy to deal with. Men—as in man, singular; and particular, as in Jared Colin. She sighed languidly, and thought, *Which only shows what dancing with a half-naked man at three o'clock in the morning in your chenille robe and satin scuffs can get you into.*

She and Jared shared cozy breakfasts in the kitchen, lunches at the Cow Café, dinners wherever fancy led them. They talked: about Katherine House, about Katherine Taggart's diary, about everything and nothing. They held hands in private moments. They kissed. The chemistry between them was explosive, and the sexual tension was mounting with each touch, each kiss, each smoldering gaze.

"He's not going to wait much longer," Caroline told Dessie. Soon they couldn't just kiss good-night and go to their separate rooms. Even if Jared would stand for it—though he hid it well with humor, his long-suffering patience was beginning to wear a little thin around the edges—Caroline couldn't go on much longer in this limbo of indecision.

"He's building up steam like a volcano about to erupt," she informed her cat, and then sighed again before confessing, "And so am I."

Caroline frowned at Dessie as though it were Dessie and not Jared Colin who'd filled her with tension and made her ache for fulfillment. Then she said, with resolve, "I've got better things to do than rub your hairy chest! I'm going to go look at wallpaper for a while."

She felt the cat's muscles tense under her fingertips just before Dessie leaped up. Every hair on the cat's body stood on end, forming a ridge along her arched spine. She growled menacingly, from deep in her throat, then hissed violently.

"Dessie? What's wrong?" Caroline reached for the cat, but Desdemona took off like a streak of black-and-white lightning. "I didn't mean—"

She stopped in midsentence, silenced by the sound of music suddenly floating down from the Kaleidoscope Room. Her scalp prickled as she recognized the melody: "Three O'Clock in the Morning."

But who—? No one could have entered the house and gotten to the Kaleidoscope Room since Jared left. She would have heard them. Had someone slipped in while she and Jared were away? But surely they would have heard his car being parked, the door opening and closing—

A chill shimmied up her spine. They'd heard it all: the car arriving home, the door opening as they came in, the door opening again as Jared left, the car leaving. Had they been up there, terrified of being caught? Had they heard the doors, the car, and heaved a sigh of relief, feeling safe—safe enough to play the Victrola again?

She shook her head, as though to dislodge the cobwebs of panic that made everything seem unfocused and illogical. Anyone who'd heard the car leave would surely have heard her talking to Dessie. *And realized she was alone? Someone who didn't fear a woman? Someone brazen enough to play the Victrola as a dare?*

Dashing into her suite, she locked the door behind her and dived across the bed to reach the phone. With trembling fingers, she punched in 9-1-1, then counted the rings, five in all, until a voice finally asked if there was an emergency. "There's someone upstairs," she blurted, then felt stupid when the operator asked for her address. "It's Katherine House," she said. "Everyone knows where it is."

"We'll send a car," the operator replied, but Caroline wasn't listening. She was listening instead to the tinkle of laughter filtering through the ceiling. A sense of déjà vu overwhelmed her. The laughter was familiar—hauntingly familiar. Almost as if in a trance, Caroline distractedly put the receiver back in its cradle. From above her came the shuffle of dancing feet, more laughter, murmurs of voices, male and female.

A minute passed. Two minutes. Three. The music slowed and faded to oblivion. She'd heard it fade that way before. Twice. Once when she'd danced with Jared, then later that same evening when the trespassers had been in the Kaleidoscope Room. Would a particular Victrola, wound to maximum tension, play exactly the same length of time, reach the same bar of music, before winding down? She grasped at the promising theory, but was forced to let it go when she remembered that the Victrola played two and half records before winding down. The odds of it winding down at the same exact spot on a particular record were so slim as to be infinitesimal.

Did it matter? She didn't know. She was too upset. She walked to the door and pressed her ear against it, hoping to hear the sounds of footfalls on the stairs, of intruders leaving. But the only thing she heard were the same intimate sounds as before: the sighing, the heavy breathing, the rhythmic thumping and urgent scrapings of lovemaking.

Caroline pressed her hands over her ears. A week ago she'd believed it was Jared upstairs—Jared and another woman. Now she didn't know what to believe, what to do. Play Sousa again?

You're hysterical, she told herself, and forced herself to draw in a deep, calming breath and exhale it slowly—then inhaled again sharply at the heavy knock that reverberated through the house. The police, she realized, at the front door. If she didn't answer, they'd probably break in.

Her hand shook as she fought with the old-fashioned key to the door of her suite. The aged lock yielded with a mechanical clunk that echoed through the room—through sudden, vast, vacuous silence.

Pressing her forehead against the door, Caroline shivered uncontrollably. Whoever was upstairs must have heard the knocking, too. Yet the silence was absolute. There was no movement at all, no scurrying one might expect of a couple scrambling for clothes, no running footfalls on the stairs. Nothing. Just an ominous lack of sound or activity.

Hoping to beat them to the stairs, hoping against hope that she didn't run headlong into them in the second-floor hallway, she flung open the door and ran as fast as she could, through the wide hall, down the stairs, across the corner of the Grand Salon to the front door. Damn Jared and his new, secure locks. She fumbled for what seemed like hours before getting the door open.

Two uniformed officers stood on the veranda. "On the third floor," she said, tilting her head to indicate the stairs.

Upon reaching the second floor, the first of the officers, a craggy-faced, barrel-chested man of about forty who looked as though he could hold his own in a bar brawl, paused to consider the narrow stairs that led to the Kaleidoscope Room.

"Holy jeez!" he told his partner in confidential tones. "There's not much room to maneuver."

"If somebody's in there, they're treed like a possum," his partner replied. He was younger, with a boyish face.

"Let's just hope he's not armed."

They drew their weapons. The gesture seemed so inappropriate to Katherine House, to Taggartville, to the boy-faced rookie officer, that Caroline found it alarming.

"You'd better step back, ma'am. In fact, you might be better off waiting downstairs." This, from the older cop, who was obviously in charge.

"I'll wait on this floor," she said, indicating the second-floor hallway. *I can't believe this is happening. Any of it.* A vision of two impulsive, hormone-driven, terrified teenagers flitted through her mind. "I don't think they... whoever's up there... is dangerous."

"Your mouth to God's ear, lady," said the seasoned cop. He didn't appear any more comfortable wielding the gun than Caroline felt watching him, and she wondered how often Taggartville's finest had to draw their weapons. She was considering telling him about the dancing and laughter and lovemaking when he precluded it by asking, "Is that door locked?"

"Not usually. But it sticks."

"Jolly," said the cop with a frown. He waved the tip of the gun to indicate Caroline should make herself scarce. She went to her suite, leaving the door open a crack so she could see and hear.

"Taggartville Police. We're coming in. Stand up and place your hands on your heads."

He repeated the advisory, then the door creaked as he twisted the knob. There were no sounds at all from the Kaleidoscope Room. Caroline was quite sure she would have heard any footsteps, even any crawling around. She held her breath—then released it with a screech when something brushed against the backs of her thighs.

Shaking, she sighed like a deflating balloon. "Dessie! You scared me to death." She picked up the cat, experiencing a sudden need to make contact with some other living thing. She massaged Dessie's head, and Dessie purred. It was the most reassuring sound Caroline had heard all night. "You shouldn't scare me like that," she whispered. "Cats may have nine lives, but I'm a human being. I've only got one."

Purposeful footsteps overhead drew her back to the immediate situation. She peeped through the crack in the door.

The older cop came into view as he left the Kaleidoscope Room and walked halfway down the stairs. "Ma'am?"

Caroline stepped into the hall. "Yes?"

"There doesn't seem to be anybody up there."

"But—" It was impossible. No one could have gotten away without her hearing.

Unless they sneaked down to the second floor and hid while you were answering the door.

Buck naked?

Intent on seeing for herself that the Kaleidoscope Room was empty, Caroline walked toward the stairs. She'd forgotten she was carrying Desdemona, until the cat suddenly howled and catapulted out of her arms, disappearing in a black-and-white blur.

"Your cat always that skittish?" the cop asked.

"She doesn't react well to strangers," Caroline said lamely. *But she's never minded strangers before.* Her mind suddenly made the connection between Dessie's odd behavior earlier and the events in the Kaleidoscope Room.

As she trailed the cop into the Kaleidoscope Room Caroline knew, beyond a doubt, that no one had been there listening to music, dancing, laughing, making love. The stylus of the Victrola was bent back in its rest position, and the turntable was empty. The clipboard she'd been using for her inventory of the room was on the window seat, exactly where she'd left it. Nothing was out of place—not a drawer, not a window, not a piece of bric-a-brac, not even the cushions she'd removed from the window seats and stacked in the middle of the floor.

The young cop shrugged his shoulders sympathetically when he saw her perplexed expression.

"Why don't you tell us what you heard," his partner said. The tone of his voice betrayed skepticism developed over years of investigating false alarms and imagined intruders.

"I thought—" Caroline began, then sighed. "I heard something moving around. It must have been mice. Dessie—my cat—killed one the other night."

"Wouldn't be surprised, old house like this," the cop said. His eyes made an evaluative survey of the room. "I always wondered what this house looked like inside. There's all kinds of stories, you know."

"Yes," Caroline agreed. "The house has a fascinating history."

"You must be the decorator Mr. Colin brought in."

She nodded.

"Didn't realize you were living here."

"In the old master suite on the second floor." Not liking the insinuation in the way the cop was looking at her, she added pointedly, "Mr. Colin's rooms are on the first floor."

"He's not here, huh?"

"He had a meeting."

"These old houses—" He tilted his head back to study the stained-glass dome, then returned his gaze to her face. "They all creak and groan."

Caroline was glad that she hadn't told him about the music and the sounds of lovemaking. Having him think she was an easily spooked female was preferable to having him think that she was a love-starved spinster fantasizing about intruders having sex in the cupola.

"Smells like flowers up here," the rookie cop said.

"Some old perfume got spilled," Caroline explained. But she'd noticed it, too—the scent of lavender that hung heavily in the air. A week had passed since she'd knocked over the perfume bottle, and the windows had been opened several times. The scent of the perfume should long since have dissipated, yet it seemed stronger. That cloyingly sweet odor— the only thing amiss in the room—sent shivers up her spine.

"We'll need some information for our report."

"We'd be more comfortable in the kitchen where we can sit down," Caroline suggested. She didn't want them in her suite—in this house—with their curious eyes any longer; she just wanted them gone.

Grudgingly she offered to make coffee, and was relieved when they declined.

Their questions were basic: her name, the address of the house, a telephone number where she could be reached if there were additional questions. The veteran cop wrote the information in a notebook, then asked, "You say you heard scuffling sounds on the third floor?"

"Yes," she replied, knowing the partial truth would be explained away by scurrying mice and a hysterical female.

The officer scribbled some more on the form, then closed the notebook. "That ought to do it."

Caroline thanked them for coming, but didn't accompany them to the door. Instead, she stayed in the kitchen and made herself a cup of hot chocolate, then sipped it slowly, trying to make sense of what had happened.

She hadn't analyzed what she'd heard a week ago. She'd believed, at the time, that it was Jared she heard; Jared and another woman. While that possibility was loathsome, it was rational. *Human.*

But what about tonight? Sounds, with no human beings to produce them. Sounds identical to the ones she'd heard the week before. The laughter and sighs of long-dead lovers destined to act out a rare moment of happiness over and over again, like a tape playing and replaying? There was no other explanation.

Except . . . unless— Stunned, Caroline set her mug of chocolate on the table with a thunk. *Like a tape playing and replaying. A tape. A sound track!* Fueled by rage and hysteria, she charged out of the kitchen. Upstairs, she frantically searched for the battery-powered lantern she'd been using in the storage room. Finding it, she also grabbed a stepladder and carried both to the Kaleidoscope Room.

Unsure what she was searching for—wires, speakers, electronic beams of light—she scoured every inch of the room within her reach: along the baseboards and around the doorjambs, behind the larger pieces of furniture, *in* the larger pieces of furniture. Nothing. Satisfied that she'd seen everything visible to the naked eye, she carried the lantern and ladder downstairs and did the same thing in her suite, paying particular attention to the ceiling. The music, the scraping, everything she'd heard, had all seemed to come from above. A strategically-placed speaker—

The intricately-carved wainscoting was next. The futility of the search overwhelmed her, cloaking her in desperation. How easy it would be to miss a tiny microphone or speaker in the multitude of niches and grooves.

Damn you, Jared Colin!

"Caroline?" Jared's voice held a trace of panic as he shouted her name from below.

Panic, she thought, listening to his footsteps on the stairs. *Nice try, Jared.* But through her stoic rage, she felt a sliver of doubt, and the beam of the lantern wobbled on the wall, reflecting the tremor of her hands.

As he came into view and caught sight of her, whole and well and perched on the stepladder, she wanted to believe that the concern he expressed was real. Jared wasn't a man prone to panic or even discomposure, but he appeared to have fallen victim to both in that moment.

Then she realized that his clothes and hair were as impeccable as ever; it was his confidence that had slipped and fallen into disarray—that cocky confidence that sent him out into the world armed with the assurance that nothing bad could happen to him because he was Jared Colin, rich boy, governor's grandson. He appeared, in that moment of panic, to have come nose-to-nose with the possibility that something could have breached his invulnerability, that there were things in the world over which he had no control and which might threaten him—*him*, and those for whom he assumed responsibility.

There was no way he could fake that, she thought, and then corrected herself: *You've fallen in love with him; you want to believe him. You want to believe in him.* She switched off the lantern, but remained on the ladder.

"Jake Thorne said he'd seen a black-and-white cruiser in front of the house."

"Good news travels fast in a town like Taggartville."

"The front door was unlocked. You left the goddamned front door unlocked!"

"I must have forgotten to lock it after the cops left."

"For God's sake, Caroline! What's been going on here?"

"I think you know what's been going on," she said coolly.

"Get down off that ladder before you break your bloody neck. What are you doing up there, anyway?"

"I think you know that, too." But she climbed off the ladder.

Jared gave a frustrated growl. "Here we go again. Jared, the clairvoyant. All-seeing. All-knowing. Psychic."

Forming his hands into fists, he faced her with a thunderous expression on his face. Caroline noted, with growing apprehension, that his nostrils actually flared when he breathed.

Then, being Jared Colin, he did the unexpected. He held up his forefingers, crooking and wiggling them in front of her face. "Here they are, Caroline. My antennae. I'm not psychic, I'm a space alien with telepathic powers. In my universe, we don't need language. We transfer thoughts."

Pressing his thumbs against the sides of his head, he wiggled the forefingers. "Do-do-de-doop. Do-do-de-doop. I'm picking up brain waves. Yes, something happened. Something definitely happened here tonight, something drastic enough to provoke you into calling the cops. Do-do-de-doop!"

Frowning, he dropped his hands. "There must be some atmospheric disturbance in here. Some Karmic imbalance. I just can't seem to grasp the details." His gaze grew ugly and accusative. "It must be that arctic wind you're fanning my way."

Caroline stiffened, armoring herself against his charm. "I heard it again, Jared. All of it. Exactly the same as last week. The music. The dancing. The heavy breathing. The—"

"Carnal escapade?"

"Don't ridicule me!" Caroline snapped. "The point is, I heard it, all of it, exactly the same."

"You can't think I circled back and sneaked into the house with the girl of the week."

She gave him a quelling scowl. "If I'd thought that, I'd have just marched upstairs and cheerfully throttled you and not bothered with the police."

"The same intruders as last time?"

"I thought they'd heard you leave for the meeting and thought we were both gone. So I locked myself in my room and called 9-1-1."

"Good girl."

Caroline drew in a deep breath. "I don't want your praise."

"How clumsy of me to compliment you on your good sense."

"The cops came in with their big, threatening guns, and shouted for whoever was in there to come out with their hands up."

She stopped. Jared waited for her to go on. When she didn't, he prompted impatiently, "Well?"

"There was no one there, Jared. No one was in the room." Her voice was flat, but the flatness was somehow accusatory. And ominous.

"The Kaleidoscope Room smelled like lavender. The cop noticed it. And so, I thought, maybe it wasn't human beings up there, maybe it was ghosts. Maybe it was Katherine and Samuel, dancing and making love."

She was scaring him. Her voice was taut with controlled emotion and she was tense, visibly tense. "Caroline—"

"I thought about them, poor Katherine and Samuel, up there in the Kaleidoscope Room, reliving the same scene over and over, dancing to the same music. And that's when I re-alized—it had struck me before, the sameness of the music, the whispering, the sighs. The sameness. Like a tape, play-ing and replaying."

Jared finally grasped her insinuation. "So here you are, searching for wires and speakers."

"How did you do it, Jared? Did your moviemaker friend help you? Did you enjoy thinking it up, getting the scenario just right? Did you have fun auditioning actors to see who could make the most passionate noises?"

Jared's throat was too tight to enable him to answer the al-legations. That she could believe he'd be so callous—

"When?" she demanded, her voice finally showing some intensity of emotion. "Did you decide to do it before I got here? Did you put me in Katherine House, so I'd be the per-fect witness for your ghosts? Or did you think of it later, when we were joking about how good a ghost would be for busi-ness."

"That's it, Caroline. The whole thing is a publicity stunt." His sarcasm grew straight out of pain, and had a rapier-sharp edge. "Did you find the speakers?"

Caroline's shoulders sagged. "No."

"How hard did you look, Caroline? It's tricky, you know. With microchip technology, everything's so small. You might miss something. Come on, let's look together." He grabbed her hand. "I think I have a magnifying glass down in my office. Let's go get it and take a second look."

"No!" she said, trying to pull her hand free.

"What's wrong, Caroline? Don't you want to find the incriminating evidence?"

"Jared—"

"What's that, I hear? Doubt? You believe I set you up, don't you? That I staged some elaborate audio drama so you'd think the house was haunted?"

"I don't know!" And she didn't. The premise had seemed so rational, so inevitable when she thought of it; but now, facing Jared, seeing his concern for her, it seemed absurd to accuse him of anything so deliberately cruel. The idea of a tape recorder and a couple of speakers—so ordinary, so linked to reality—had been appealing. Far more so than the idea of ghosts.

Jared released her hand, tossing it away from him as though touching it were repugnant. "I want you out of my house."

"Jared—"

"I'll pay off your contract, plus lodging tonight and two nights on the road back to Massachusetts."

"You're firing me?" It was incomprehensible.

"There are several hotels just this side of Orlando. I'll call around to find one with a vacancy while you're packing."

"Tonight?"

"No relationship works without trust, Caroline. Professional or personal. I thought we had both, but it appears we have neither."

He turned to leave, determined to make a clean exit without a backward glance. If he hesitated, he would weaken.

"I do trust you."

The words, spoken softly, paralyzed Jared. Knowing he'd be lost if he looked at her, he looked anyway. Caroline appeared small, and vulnerable and broken. He'd never wanted to protect and comfort a woman as desperately as he wanted to take her into his arms at that moment. He'd never needed to feel a woman's arms around him more than he needed to be wrapped in her gentle embrace.

"Jared, I'm scared," she said.

9

JARED, I'M SCARED. A plea. Three little words—perhaps the only combination of words in the English language capable, at that moment, of reaching past Jared's injured ego, past his indignant rage at having been falsely accused, to touch his heart.

Jared, I'm scared. Three little words that set off every protective male instinct he possessed. Five running steps brought him to her, and she was in his arms instantly, hugging him not gently, but fiercely.

He buried his face in her hair, feeling its silky texture against his skin, inhaling its clean scent. *I was scared, too,* he thought. *Terrified for your safety. Terrified of losing you.*

"I don't want to believe in ghosts," Caroline said. Jared felt her trembling and the moisture of tears seeping through his shirt. He kissed the top of her head, stroked her back and murmured assurances in her ear.

Ghosts? Closing his eyes, Jared tried to imagine what he would think, how he would feel if he'd heard what she'd heard. He might be clinging to her for reassurance if the tables were turned. He might try to deny it, grasp for logical explanations.

Caroline made a snuffling noise and burrowed her cheek against his chest. Jared responded by hugging her a bit tighter and thinking, sadly, *I wouldn't have doubted you.*

She was still trembling, he realized. With a disgruntled sigh, Jared picked her up and carried her to the bed. "Don't get the wrong idea," he said, as he deposited her on the comforter. "It's the only comfortable piece of furniture in sight."

He joined her, sliding his arm under her neck and letting gravity do the rest. Her head settled in the cradle of his arm, and she draped her arm across his chest and sighed. Her hip pressed against his, and their legs aligned cozily.

Neither spoke, and Caroline grew so still, her breathing so even, that Jared wondered if she'd fallen asleep. But at length, she whispered, "Do you think I'm crazy?"

"I think you're wonderful," he said, and kissed the top of her head. *But I wish you trusted me more.*

"Do you believe in ghosts?"

"I've never given it much thought." *But I believe in you— why couldn't you have believed in me?*

"It doesn't make any sense."

"What doesn't?"

"Katherine's ghost in the Kaleidoscope Room. I did a paper on ghost lore in college. Ghosts haunt the place they died, not where they lived."

"If she's dancing and laughing and making love, maybe she's reliving happy memories."

"That's just it. Spirits don't linger on earth to relive happy memories. They become earthbound when there's something unresolved at the time of death—usually some sort of violence. Sometimes it happens so suddenly that they become confused, and don't know they're dead. Katherine should be walking the scene of the train wreck, not dancing in the Kaleidoscope Room."

"That's a glum thought—that ghosts stick around because of violence or trauma, but not because of love."

"That sounded dangerously close to a romantic sentiment," Caroline said.

"I'm not the callous bastard you insist on thinking I am."

She tensed. Jared felt the sudden tension in her body. "I'm sorry about . . . earlier."

Jared abruptly rolled onto his side, and braced his arm on the other side of her. His face hovered inches above hers.

"Look at me, Caroline. You've danced with me at three o'clock in the morning. You've kissed me. You must know—sense—that I care about you. How could you believe that I would be so deliberately cruel in order to use you?"

"I wasn't thinking straight."

"I don't know how you could have thought it at all."

She closed her eyes and turned her head to the side. Her hair fell across her face, hiding it.

"Maybe it's Taggart," Jared said. "He died in the house. Maybe he's reliving the last night he spent with Katherine. Maybe they danced and laughed and made love, and then she left for Tallahassee and never came back. That could have been *his* turmoil at death. Maybe he mourned her so intensely that his love for her brought her back to him in death."

Caroline's eyes sprang open in surprise. "Is this coming from the man who said Taggart moved downstairs because his joints were stiff?"

"That was when I was young and naive."

She smiled gently. "Almost two weeks ago."

Jared brushed the hair from her face. "I'm furious with you, and yet...looking at you, I can understand why a man could become obsessed with spending eternity with a woman."

Caroline tried to speak, but Jared's name stuck in her throat. Her face warmed under his gaze, and the hunger in his eyes sent tendrils of heat curling through her body. She raised her hands to cradle his face, and met that hungry gaze directly. Her own eyes were liquid with emotion. "I didn't mean to hurt you."

Her eyes drifted shut as he lowered his face to hers. His mouth fused over hers with a devastating blend of intensity and tenderness, and claimed her, heart and soul, with a blend of plunder and gentle seduction. The kiss was at once violent with yearning, and soothing with the promise of fulfillment.

Caroline slid her arms around his neck to pull him closer, loving the strength that emanated from his body, the weight of his chest against her breasts. He tore his mouth from hers to burrow his face at the juncture of her neck and jaw. His breath, hot and moist, fanned over her sensitive skin. "I should have kicked you out," he said. "Now look what's happening."

"I'll leave, if that's what you want."

He hugged her to him fiercely. "It's too late, Sugar Lips. Don't even think it."

Caroline sighed raggedly. "I've done too much thinking tonight. Right now, I want to quit thinking and just feel."

"You should quit thinking more often," Jared told her. "You have your best ideas that way."

He kissed her with a fervor that stole her breath away and drove all rational thought from her mind. He was a skilled lovemaker, as she'd known he would be; tender, thorough, at times patient and giving, at times impatient and demanding. Caroline surrendered herself to the oblivion of sensation, cooperating as he unbuttoned buttons and struggled with clasps, accepting the touch of his hands, his lips, his tongue on her flesh, encouraging him with sighs and sensual whimpers and searching, loving caresses.

Greedily, she tore at the buttons of his shirt and shoved the fronts aside, then explored the contrasts of him—hard sinew, smooth muscle and fine, dark hair. She kissed him, tasted his skin, drew on his flat nipples with her mouth until they peaked, pebblelike, against her lips and a groan of arousal sounded from Jared's throat. Then she moved, guiding his chest to hers, so that the sprinkling of hair there chafed her breasts, and then pressed him closer, so that her breasts compressed against his less pliant chest muscles, relishing his warmth, his strength.

She kissed his neck and nibbled on his ear while exploring his back with her hands, kneading and stroking. Bending her knee, she draped her leg over his. Jared cupped her hips and pulled her to him, cradling her against his hardness, letting her feel his erection. Caroline clung to him, groaning softly and anointing his neck and shoulders with tiny kisses.

They held each other for measureless minutes, adjusting to the new level of intimacy between them, delirious with sensation, enthralled by anticipation. Caroline insinuated her fingers past the waistband of Jared's pants and kneaded his buttocks, teasing and taunting. With a sensual groan, Jared captured her wrists and drew her hands away, guiding them to the bed on either side of her head as he rolled atop her. He looked down into her face with adoration and awe, and threaded his fingers through hers, then kissed her deeply.

He blazed a trail of kisses from her mouth, along her jaw, over her neck, down to the tender hollow between her breasts. He rested his head there for several seconds before releasing her hands and rolling aside, bracing his weight on his left elbow while he undid the hook and zipper of her pants with his right hand.

Caroline fought the opening of his trousers at the same time, progressing with frustrating slowness on a perversely stubborn zipper with her trembling fingers. Jared dispatched her pants, then reached down to help her, smiling when their gazes met. "I know you're anxious, Sugar Lips, but you're going to kill me if you keep this up."

He remembered the condom in his billfold before tossing his trousers aside. As he sat on the edge of the bed with his back to her, donning it, Caroline sat up and tortured him, playfully nipping his collarbone with her teeth while her breasts teased his shoulders in featherlike brushes as she moved.

"Vixen!" Jared turned quickly and pushed her down on the bed, rolling atop her again to trap her there.

"You should have thrown me out while you had the chance," she answered huskily.

"I'd rather torture you instead," he rasped, but his treatment of her was anything but abusive as he kissed, tasted, teased, stroked and tantalized.

Ultimately their joining was gentle. Caroline moaned as he entered her body, awed by the rightness of it, the almost-unbearable intensity of sensual ecstasy their union brought. Slowly, tentatively, Jared began moving, and she moved with him, following his lead, her body and her need attuned to his as though they'd been lovers for many years.

Jared experienced a totally new physical completeness as he slid into her softness. She was warm and sweet, and the pleasure of being absorbed by her left him momentarily breathless. Her legs—those long legs he'd admired from the first time he saw her—were locked around his, drawing him closer, anchoring him snugly to her. When he moved against her, inside her, Caroline instinctively moved with him, tightening her legs as she thrust upward with her hips.

Time and logic lost their relevance as Jared surrendered to release from the tension inside him. He yearned for that release, needed it with a fierce, frightening intensity. The sounds she made, purring moans of encouragement, fueled the fire inside him. He heard those moans, and the guttural, desperate cries that echoed his own urgency; he felt her body uncoiling, caressing him in spasms of climax while she arched against him and tightened her legs around him. She was both vulnerable and strong as she clung to him, her hands clutching the muscles of his back.

He thrust again, again, and yet again, cradling her hips in his hands, rocking her with him, taking her with him as he toppled over the edge into his own climax. Depleted, sated, he drew her as close as physically possible and clung to her as desperately as she had clung to him.

His next conscious awareness was of fleeting kisses on his forehead. They settled like butterflies on a blossom, then moved on to a new spot. Surprised he had energy enough to smile, he did, pushing up on his arms so that his face hovered inches above hers. "You're beating a dead horse, Sugar Lips."

He felt her midsection vibrate as she laughed softly. "A dead stallion?"

Jared grinned. "A *dormant* stallion. It takes a while for the batteries to recharge after a gallop like that."

Caroline brushed his hair off his forehead. "You're mixing your metaphors. And I wasn't trying to start anything." *I was trying to show you that what we shared was special.*

"Liar!"

"Insensitive, egotistical male!"

He bristled—as well as a man could bristle so soon after being totally drained of strength by incredible sex—and eased off her, grimacing at having to give up the intimacy of their bonding. "What'd I do to deserve that?"

"Nothing." Caroline closed her eyes and sighed. "You were just being a man."

"And I got the distinct impression you were enjoying it," Jared said drolly.

"As a matter of fact, I was . . . did." She leaned over to kiss his nose, then his chin. "Let's do it again."

Jared groaned. "I'd love to, Sugar Lips, but it would be a physical impossibility."

"A stallion like you?" she teased. "Let's check." She became a temptress, kissing, nipping, tickling. Her hands went lower to slide around his thighs and slip between, tantalizing.

"Ye gods, Caroline!" Jared said. "Have some compassion!"

"Compassion is not in my vocabulary! Ah, just as I thought—it's not impossible, after all."

Jared groaned. "You should be flattered."

"That's not all I am."

He captured her wrist. "Slow down, Sugar Lips. I haven't even taken care of the first time, and I don't have the energy to go trotting downstairs for supplies."

"You don't have to do that," she said, smiling with all the sly innocence of a schoolgirl making a naughty suggestion.

That grin again, cocky and cocksure. It melted Caroline's heart and set her blood racing as Jared cradled her face in his hands. "I could probably make it to the bathroom and back," he said, as though making a supreme sacrifice.

"I'll take care of the supplies," she offered, in the same spirit of sacrifice.

He kissed her briefly on the lips. "I love a woman who's responsible as well as beautiful."

Love. It tumbled off his tongue easily—so easily that Caroline felt her heart contract a bit at the casual way he dropped it, as though it were as inconsequential as a used paper towel or a piece of junk mail.

I love a woman. . . . Woman, general. Nonspecific. Caroline lay back on the pillow and frowned. *Trust a politician to speak in generalities.*

By the time Jared returned, strutting in his altogether as though he were accustomed to strolling around buck naked, she had folded back the comforter and was propped up against the pillows with the sheet pulled up under her chin. She motioned to the vacant side of the bed where the sheet was turned back invitingly. "Welcome back, honey buns."

"Does this mean I get to stay awhile?" Jared asked as he climbed in beside her.

"I was hoping you'd think of that," she said, cuddling next to him. "I could use a more substantial bedfellow than Desdemona tonight."

"Me, too, Sugar Lips," he said, quite sincerely. She felt delicious next to him, lush and woman-soft. Her hair smelled like spring breezes and the hollow of her neck—she must have put on fresh perfume. He would have been content just to lie there holding her all night, but that hadn't been the agenda, and with her breasts wedged against his ribs, and her thigh resting across his, he was more than ready to resume where they'd left off.

"Where's the sex-starved seductress I left?" he asked.

"Right under your nose," Caroline purred. With a few subtle movements, she was stretched full-length atop him, threading her fingers in his hair and driving him crazy with nibbling kisses all over his face. Her hair fell forward to tease his shoulders.

"I'm very glad I didn't kick you out tonight," he murmured, then captured her head in his hands and guided her mouth to his.

It was like putting match to kerosene. This time there were no clothes to dispatch, no first-time awkwardness to impede their lovemaking. The memory, mental and tactile, of what they'd shared earlier added a new dimension to their touching. Jared let Caroline set the pace, and she alternated between slow and frenzied, captivating him with her frank appreciation of his body and the pleasure their lovemaking brought to her.

The culmination this time was as cataclysmic as before and even more physically consuming. As they lay there, holding each other, sated, replete with the pleasure they'd given each other, silence was more communicative than any words ever could have been, and even more so were the gentle nudges of flesh against flesh and the respondent soft sighs.

Jared kissed her on the ear and hugged her gently before extricating himself from her embrace and the tangle of bed linens to make the necessary pilgrimage to the bathroom. When he returned and spooned his body against hers, she snuggled close and sighed and was asleep within seconds. Jared lay awake a bit longer—minutes perhaps—wondering at the fullness he felt in his heart. All tension had drained from his body, and the world seemed as far away as a distant universe, totally irrelevant. Physically, he was exhausted; yet, as he cradled Caroline in his arms, his mind and heart reverberated with an emotional energy that radiated contentment and well-being.

Her hair was spread over the pillow near his face, and he went to sleep breathing in the springtime scent of Caroline's hair.

CAROLINE FELL INTO A DEEP sleep. Except for an occasional unconscious snuggle and accompanying murmur of contentment, she slept soundly until just past five in the morning.

Disoriented at first, she opened her eyes to the predawn darkness, unsure where she was or why there was a warm, solid presence next to her. Then she roused enough to remember the night before. She smiled as she noted Jared's right arm under her neck and his left crooked possessively around her waist.

"Cat!" The anguished cry, so close to her ear, startled her. The arm around her waist flexed, gripping her with a vise-like determination. Jared groaned, tossed and fought in his sleep.

"No, no!" He shouted the words as though beholding and denying a scene from hell. "Cat, no!"

Caroline soothed him, stroked him, told him everything would be all right, but he fought her comfort and assurances, still calling out desperate denials in his sleep before giving one final, plaintive "No-o-o." The tension drained from his body, and his arm relaxed into a dead weight across Caroline's waist, and Caroline realized he'd never awakened during the nightmare.

She lay there, unable to go back to sleep, and listened to his even breathing, resenting the fact that he was sleeping like a baby and she was wide-awake at five-thirty in the morning.

What nightmare haunted his sleep, stalked his dreams? The first time he'd said cat, she'd pictured a housecat, like Dessie. But it was obviously a name.

Cat—Short for Cathy? Or Catherine?

He'd been dreaming about another woman! She considered giving him a swift slap on the face and pretending to be asleep when he jerked awake, then thought better of it as she succumbed to the sheer bliss of being held in his strong, male arms. After all, Jared could hardly be held accountable for a breach of etiquette committed in his sleep, even if he committed it in her bed. Which was, technically, she supposed, his bed by virtue of ownership, anyway.

She did, however, allow herself a small surge of satisfaction that the dream obviously had not been a pleasant one. Unless, of course, someone named Cat had been having her naughty way with him, in which case she doubted he would be protesting quite so vehemently.

She didn't fall asleep again and, after an hour, she grew restless. Carefully wriggling out of Jared's embrace, she pulled on her chenille robe and padded downstairs to the kitchen for orange juice and Raisin Bran. For once, she might actually get some nourishment before Jared woke up and cajoled her into one of his gooey, delectable Colin's Breads pastries.

As she ate, she reflected on the events of the night before—the music and laughter from the Kaleidoscope Room, the tense wait for the cops, the realization that no human beings were in that room, her suspicion that Jared was trying to stage a publicity stunt of some kind, the frantic concern on Jared's face when he'd come dashing upstairs demanding to know what had happened, their argument, their lovemaking, the possessive way he'd held her in his sleep, the nightmare.

She tumbled the events over and over in her mind, trying to put them into perspective, until Jared joined her, shirtless but wearing his slacks from the night before. His hair was charmingly mussed, his face still slightly marked from the creases in the pillow. The overall effect was blatantly sexy.

"I thought the aroma of coffee would get you up," she teased.

"Actually, it was your cat."

"Desdemona?" Caroline asked. "I'll bet she was surprised to see you."

"Not half as surprised as I was to see her. I felt something nudging my cheek and thought it was you. But when I opened my eyes, looking forward to a proper good-morning, I was eyeball-to-eyeball with that fur ball of yours. Her breath smells like fish."

"Tuna is her favorite flavor of cat food."

Jared took the box of pastries from the refrigerator. "Apple or raspberry?"

"Apple," she said, then watched him put them in the microwave and pour himself coffee. When they were ready, he joined her at the table.

"I've been thinking," she said.

Jared grimaced. "At least let me get a few sips of this coffee."

"It's not that bad," Caroline protested, nettled by his attitude.

"Caroline, when a woman says, 'I've been thinking,' in that tone of voice, it's bad. And when she says it before seven o'clock in the morning, it's bound to be awful."

The silence grew overlong as she waited for him to drink his coffee. Finally Jared set aside his mug and looked at her, then stretched his arms across the table so that he could cradle her face in his. "You're beautiful in the morning."

"Flatterer," Caroline accused, but she said it without rancor.

Jared was uncharacteristically somber. "You're not having second thoughts about last night, are you? You're not sorry?"

"Not about making love with you," she replied.

"Thank God," he said, with a sigh of relief, and reached for his mug again.

"I was thinking about ghosts."

"After last night, I'd rather have hoped you'd be thinking about me."

"I was thinking about you, too. It's all linked together. There's a sequence. Jared, we triggered the ghosts."

"Maybe you'd better go a little slower. The caffeine hasn't had time to kick in yet."

"Concentrate, Jared. The sequence. The song on the Victrola. 'Three O'Clock in the Morning.' Then laughter. Then dancing. Then kissing. We did all that last week, the day you brought the Victrola home."

Jared nodded. "I'm with you so far."

"What if—Jared, what if Katherine and Samuel did the same thing. What if they played the same record, and laughed and danced and kissed, then—"

"We didn't make love that day."

"No. We didn't go that far. But the mood was the same. Romantic and frivolous. And that night, I heard them replaying the scenario. That's one reason I was so incensed. I thought you were working the same routine on another woman, playing the Victrola, dancing, kissing."

"It wasn't a routine!"

"I know that now," she assured him. "It was a perfectly logical sequence of events with two people who are attracted to each other. It was just . . . the same room, the same record, the same emotions. And I knocked over the perfume bottle."

"That lavender stuff?"

Caroline nodded. "Katherine's perfume. The scent of it was strong last night. The cop noticed it. And you noticed it the day we danced."

"Is that significant?"

"Ghosts often are associated with scents. The fact that the scent was there, in the air, when we cranked up the Victrola—" A pregnant silence ensued, during which she locked her gaze with his. "Jared, if we did somehow . . . bring them back, how do we—?"

"Put them back to rest?"

She nodded. Jared exhaled a defeated sigh. "Damned if I know."

They fell into a thoughtful silence, which Caroline eventually broke by asking, "Do you remember dreaming last night?"

His gaze grew warm as he reached for her hand. "I *lived* a dream last night."

Caroline couldn't help smiling. "You're sweet, Jared, but I meant after you went to sleep."

"Why do you ask?"

Attempting nonchalance, Caroline rose and walked to the coffeepot to refill her mug. "Katherine's a very formal name. Do you suppose the people close to her ever shortened it? Like, to Kathy?"

"My grandfather called her Kath."

Kath—not Kat, Caroline reflected. She sat down and took a sip of coffee. "Katherine's a very common name. I guess everyone has known a Kathy, or a Kat."

"I suppose so," Jared agreed.

"Did you ever date a Katherine?"

"Did you ever date a Thomas or a James?"

Touché! Caroline thought.

Noting the frustration on Caroline's face, Jared asked, "Does this have anything to do with the dream question earlier?"

"You had a nightmare last night, Jared. You called out for someone named Cat." *Or, Kat.*

"I was probably dreaming about that fur ball of yours."

"It was a name." She put her hand on his forearm imploringly. "Jared, this isn't jealousy, or female curiosity. I'm not trying to invade your privacy. It could be...relevant. If there was someone in your past named Cat, then the dream was perfectly normal."

"And if there wasn't—" Jared mused.

"Samuel might have called her Kat," Caroline said. "We talked about the fact that ghosts only haunt the place of their death, and that it could be Samuel's—" she searched for a word "—*energy* up there. While you were dreaming, you were thrashing about. You sounded...troubled. If Samuel called Katherine Kat—"

Jared drew away from her, pulling his arm out of her grasp as he sat back in his chair. He took a steeling breath. "What you're suggesting borders on possession."

"Not possession," she said. "Just...energy. Emotion. You were in Samuel's bed, in Samuel's room. You could have been picking up on that energy like a radio receiver."

"The same way you're picking up on Katherine?"

Caroline bowed her head, realizing, for the first time, how alone she was in this situation. She was the only person who'd heard anything supernatural from the Kaleidoscope Room. Jared had heard Sousa, and the cops had opened the Kaleidoscope Room door to silence. She winced slightly. *Dead* silence. Silence and the scent of lavender. How significant was that lavender scent? Couldn't a bottle of dried-up perfume leak an odor like that? With the door closed, it could build up. Maybe there was nothing at all supernatural about the scent of lavender. Maybe there had never been any sounds in that room. Maybe they had existed only in the mind of the only person who heard them.

"Do you think I'm imagining what I heard?" she asked in words as soft as puffs of cotton.

"Why would you do that?"

Caroline lifted her head so she could see his face. He sounded so calm, so reasonable—the voice of reason in the midst of uncertainty.

"You've been enchanted by Katherine's story from the beginning, but it was a healthy curiosity," he continued. He reached across the table to cup her chin in his fingertips. "You're no lonely, impressionable woman, Caroline. You have a life of your own. Why would you need hers, especially when you have access to her diaries, her room, to everything she owned?"

A ragged sigh tore from her throat. "I wish you'd heard it, too."

"So do I."

He meant it; and Caroline found his loyalty overwhelmingly sweet. "Will you hold me?" she asked.

Jared rose and guided her into his arms. "It's about time I got that proper good-morning."

There was oblivion in his embrace as well as pleasure. Caroline let it enfold her, salving her mind while her body responded to him physically. She surrendered all thought as he kissed her, deeply and thoroughly.

"Now I finally get to find out what you wear under this Victorian virtue-defender," Jared said, slipping his hand inside the wrap fronts of the chenille robe. His smile was pure dishonorable intent when he announced, "Why, Caroline, you're not wearing *anything* under your robe!"

"I didn't want to wake you up," she said huskily, as his hands roved over her bare skin.

He brushed aside the front of her robe and buried his face between her breasts. "I don't know how you do this to me."

"Do what?" she asked breathlessly, squeezing the muscles of his back in her hands as she clung to him.

"This." Cupping her buttocks, he pulled her in to his hardness.

"Oh, my!" she said, suddenly whimsical.

"I woke up wanting you," he rasped.

"For what?"

"Hold on, Sugar Lips, and I'll show you." Moving so swiftly that she didn't have time to anticipate it, he slung her over his shoulder fireman-style and carried her into his bedroom. It was an erotic journey, with her breasts swaying against his shoulder blades, his arm across the backs of her thighs, the friction created by their movement.

The water bed sloshed frantically as he dropped her onto it. Jared looked down at her as she drifted on those contained waves, her breasts marked by his beard, her nipples pebbled, one thigh covered, the other exposed by the gaping, askew robe.

He lowered himself onto the bed beside her and pushed aside the robe, untying the belt that had long since become superfluous. He ran his hand down her side, stopped with it resting lightly on her thigh, just above the knee. "You're incredible, Caroline Naylor."

Caroline smiled. "So you remember my real name."

"I haven't forgotten anything I ever learned about you— and I'm desperate to learn everything else there is to know."

He learned several interesting tidbits as they made love in the bars of morning sunlight pouring through the slats of the blinds. Her face was a fascinating visual register of the pleasure she took from their togetherness. When they were both sated, he cradled that beautiful face in his hands and kissed it all over, again and again, then lay with his body spooned against hers, and held her. Within minutes, she fell asleep, and although he was bounding with energy, as he always was in the morning, he stayed close to her a bit longer, just for the joy of looking at her face.

The next thing Caroline knew, Jared was kissing her awake. "Oh. Jared. Hi," she said, lifting her hand to cover a yawn.

Jared grinned at her grogginess and disorientation. "I would have let you sleep, but there's a Mrs. Kippirich here who says she's supposed to help with the inventory."

Clutching the sheet under her arms, Caroline sprang into a sitting position. "Oh, my gosh! Mrs. Kippirich is one of Aunt Essie's cronies from the society." She groaned. "We'll probably be written up in the next society news bulletin!"

Putting a hand on each side of her face, he kissed her briefly on the mouth. "Sugar Lips, if anyone saw your face right now, we could end up in Guinness. But relax. I told her you were running a little late. She's settled in the kitchen with coffee and a Danish. I'll keep her there while you sneak upstairs and then reemerge fresh and innocent as a daisy."

He found her robe and held it up for her, standing just far enough from the bed so that she would have to get out in her altogether in order to put it on—and he watched closely.

"Clever, aren't you?" she said.

"Just being a gentleman."

"Humph!" She adjusted the robe and tied the belt. "I can say one thing for you, Jared. You think quickly on your feet. If you ever get caught in a compromising situation with a bimbo in the middle of a campaign, I'm sure you'll find a way to smuggle her past the press without any inquiring minds finding out."

Jared wrapped his fingers around her upper arm. "I'd call a press conference and *announce* that I slept with you last night. Hell, I'd hand out press releases. It meant that much to me. I just thought that, under the circumstances, you might not want our private relationship providing fodder for the next luncheon meeting of the Taggartville Historical Preservation Society meeting."

Covering his hand with hers, she said, "You're right, of course. And I appreciate your...ability to take care of an awkward situation."

"One of these days you're going to have to tell me what it is about me that irritates you so much," he said. "But right now I need to get back to the kitchen to keep Mrs. Kippirich at bay. She thinks I'm concluding a phone call."

He preceded her out the door and signaled from the kitchen doorway that she should make her dash to the stairs. Caroline sprinted the width of the Grand Salon, then tiptoed up the stairs, wondering why—indeed—she should be so irritated with him for being clever enough to protect her reputation.

Finally, as she took what would probably have qualified as one of the fastest baths in the history of indoor bathing, she decided it must have been the mental image of Jared Colin fooling around with a bimbo in the middle of a campaign.

Jared Colin was going to make a damned good politician. Too bad she wasn't interested in playing the role of political wife he was casting.

10

CAROLINE AND Mrs. Kippirich worked on the storage-room inventory until midafternoon, stopping only long enough for a quick sandwich. Since Caroline had already cataloged most of the furniture, they concerned themselves with bric-a-brac that had been tossed in boxes or shut away in drawers. These items they sorted, as they recorded, into boxes for suggested discard or possible decorative use.

After the tedious task of inventorying, Caroline was glad to get back to her wallpaper samples, fabric swatches and paint chips. She had made preliminary sketches of each of the second-story rooms, and selected a theme and color scheme for each, and she was anxious to make her final decisions on wallpaper and window treatments.

At just after five, Jared returned from a business meeting in Orlando. Hearing him ascend the stairs, Caroline went to the landing to wait for him, and greeted him with a big kiss.

"I could get used to this." The words slipped from Jared's tongue without any conscious decision on his part, and he realized that, trite or not, he meant them more sincerely than anything witty or urbane he might have chosen to say. On the drive back from Orlando, he'd looked forward to getting home, to hugging Caroline and asking her what she'd been up to, to asking what they were doing for dinner; he'd imagined talking to her across a candlelit table while the tension mounted between them, then to making slow, sweet love before curling up together and going to sleep.

So, he thought, as he hugged her, *it's finally happened to Jared Colin.* He might have told her, if she hadn't picked that moment to pull away and, taking his hand, said, "I've got something to show you."

It was sketches and wallpaper samples and fabric swatches, and though he scarcely saw what she was pointing out or listened to her jabber about making statements with light and color, he let her jabber and pretended to be interested because her enthusiasm for her work always captivated him, and there was pleasure in watching her face as she animatedly discussed the windows and walls of his house.

"I can order the blinds and call in the paperhangers and send the furniture to the refinishers tomorrow if you'll just approve the wallpaper with the purple elephants," she concluded.

"Purple elephants?"

"Just testing," she said. "I didn't think you were hearing a word I've said."

"You want me to approve everything so you can call in the paperhangers. Where do I initial my approval?"

"It would be nice if you looked at what you're approving."

"Sorry. I'm a little distracted." *It's so much nicer looking at you.* "Why don't you go over it again."

This time, he listened. And initialed. And then pulled her into his lap and kissed her nose and said, "Tomorrow morning you can call in a whole battalion of paperhangers. Now I want you to tell me where you'd like to go for dinner."

She stiffened visibly. "Jared—"

"I *hate* it when you say my name like that."

"I'm serious."

"I know. When you say my name that way, it's like a trumpet fanfare heralding unpleasant news."

She glared at him, frowning petulantly.

"Well, spit it out!" he snapped.

"I don't know if it's a good idea for us to...monopolize each other."

"I feel a lot of things with you, Caroline. Monopolized is not one of them."

"Just because we're—"

"Lovers?"

"Involved, and living in close quarters, you don't have to be responsible for me every minute. Or every meal."

Jared frowned, but the frown gradually metamorphosed into a cocky grin. His eyes never left her face. "What if I told you there's nothing I'd rather do tonight than take you to some great little restaurant and hold your hand on top of the table and look at the reflection of candlelight dancing in your eyes?"

Caroline felt warm all over. How could a woman look into a gaze like that and not melt a little, from the inside out? "I'd say you have a date," she said.

"You're sure you didn't have other plans?" he teased. "I wouldn't want to *monopolize* your time."

"The only thing I had planned for tonight was a visit to the Taggartville library."

Jared lifted an eyebrow dubiously.

"Tonight's their late night."

"I wasn't aware Taggartville had a *late* night."

"They stay open until seven, instead of five."

"Seven o'clock. No one can say this isn't a wild and crazy town! So, is there a specific book you wanted, or do you just need something to read?"

"I could read Katherine's copy of *Topper* if I just wanted something to read. I thought I'd do some research on your great-aunt."

"Research?"

"I thought I'd look up the news accounts of the Tragic Derailment."

"We can stop on the way out of town, if you like."

"No," she said firmly. "It'll wait." She put her hands on his shoulders and looked up into his face. "I suddenly realized that I don't want to think about death tonight. Not death, or morbid accidents or ghosts—"

"What is it?" Jared asked, when she stopped abruptly.

"Nothing, really. I just happened to recall that *Topper* is about two ghosts. It's peculiar that it must have been one of Katherine's favorite books." With a small lift of her shoulders, she added, "It probably doesn't mean a thing."

"Except that maybe she believed in ghosts."

"That's not a reassuring thought."

"You mean, if Katherine believed in ghosts, it might have opened some door for her to come back as a ghost."

Caroline nodded somberly. "Yes. And if...if...that's true, and I believe that what I heard in the Kaleidoscope Room were ghosts, where does that leave me? Wandering restlessly through eternity?"

Jared tightened his arms around her and kissed the top of her head when she gratefully burrowed her cheek against his chest. "It leaves you with a long and productive life ahead of you. But first, it leaves you going out to dinner with a gorgeous hunk who adores you, and then to some mindless movie where you can forget all about this house and my great-aunt and a train derailment that happened over sixty years ago."

"I don't know any gorgeous hunks," she said drolly.

"Then you'll have to settle for me."

"I can live with that," she told him, and Jared thought, *And I could live with you for the rest of my life.*

CAROLINE BECAME SO DEEPLY involved with the mundane, wonderfully ordinary details of the renovation that she had no time to dwell on what she had or had not heard coming from the cupola, or its origins.

At night, there was Jared.

Caroline cooked dinner for him: broiled chicken breasts and rice pilaf.

Jared cooked dinner for Caroline: spaghetti and marinara sauce, served with Colin's Breads garlic breadsticks. They joked about breath sprays. They joked about vampires. And they discovered a little garlic among friends was no catastrophe.

They talked. They watched movies on his VCR. Caroline started reading *Topper*, Jared got hopelessly involved with a technothriller, and they cuddled together on his sofa and read. And they made love, sometimes slowly and sweetly, sometimes urgently, sometimes with a playfulness that demanded acrobatic skill.

After one particularly physically demanding romp, Caroline lay with her head on Jared's chest, listening to the strong pulse of his heart, and sighed. "How old are you, Jared?"

"Twenty-nine. Why?"

"Just wondering. You have so much . . . stamina."

"I hope that's a compliment."

"It is. I was just thinking about Katherine and Samuel. Katherine was the same age I was when she died. And Samuel—I figured it out—he was sixty. He probably didn't have the stamina you have."

"The man lived until he was a hundred and three. He might have been a very active sixty-year-old."

"Maybe. But being sixty years old in 1930 was not quite the same as being sixty years old today. He must have seemed ancient to Katherine."

"Not as ancient as he must have seemed when he was forty-nine and she was sixteen."

"When I was sixteen, I played Juliet in the high-school production of *Romeo and Juliet*."

Jared snickered.

Caroline wanted to be irritated but couldn't be. "It *was* pretty awful."

"I doubt that," Jared said. "I can see you as Juliet."

"Why'd you laugh?" she challenged, putting one hand atop the other on his chest and propping her chin on them so she could see his face.

"At the inevitability of it."

She lifted her head off her hands momentarily. "Inevitability?"

"You. Boston. Shakespeare. My high school staged *Grease*."

"Were you in it?"

Another chuckle. "No."

Caroline grew thoughtful again. "That seems like a million years ago. When I think of everything I've done since then—college, the European tour—"

"Of course. No self-respecting art-history major could possibly *survive* without a European tour."

"It was tourist class. I worked my fanny off to earn money for that trip."

"At an art museum."

"There's a lot of hard work to be done behind the scenes at an art museum. But we're off the subject. What I meant is, I can't imagine what it would have been like to have been married at sixteen, and to be looking back now and have been married for ten years. Age means a whole lot less now than it did then, but I've never even dated a man over forty, and I can't imagine being in bed with a sixty-year-old."

"They'd been married ten years, Caroline. Some of the glow would have worn off by then, anyway."

"She would have been on the verge of her sexual prime, although probably no one would ever have told her that in that day and age. She must have wondered what it would be like with a younger man."

"By all accounts she was absolutely devoted to Samuel."

"I didn't mean that she would ever have been unfaithful. It's obvious from her diary that she was devoted to him. But most of her references to him make him seem rather paternal. He gave her books to read, encouraged her to keep a journal—things a father would do."

"That was probably to be expected, given their ages and backgrounds."

"Still," Caroline said. "Katherine must have wondered." She laid her cheek back on his chest. "Did you know she was frustrated that she never had his child?"

"No. I didn't know."

"Apparently he wanted an heir. That must have been part of the reason he proposed to her out of the blue."

"Taggart could have proposed to any number of women over a number of years. He fell madly in love with Katherine at first sight."

Her head popped up. "I thought you said it was *lust* at first sight."

"That was before I knew what a woman could do to a man." He cradled her face in his palms. "Look how quickly I fell in love with you at twenty-nine. It might have been instantaneous if I'd had to wait until I was forty-nine to meet you."

Caroline's throat constricted. "Love?"

"Haven't I mentioned it before?" Jared asked.

"Not . . . *love*."

"It's still new to me, too."

"Jared."

"Caroline, you know how I hate it when you say my name that way."

"But Jared—*love?*"

"Surely you've heard of it, Caroline. It's the emotion that binds a man and a woman together with tenderness and magic. It's waltzing at three o'clock and not caring how late it is. It's holding a woman in your arms and knowing that she belongs there. And when a man tells a woman he's in love with her, she's supposed to say his name like a sigh, not like an answer to a summons to the dentist's chair."

His face was so close to hers that his features blurred in her vision. "I'm—" she said, but left the thought incomplete.

"Let's see if we can't work on softening up the way you say my name."

He kissed her until the world spun, and then drew only far enough away for her to see the expression of adulation in his eyes. "Say my name," he implored.

"You always get what you want, don't you, Jared?"

"Stubborn wench! Say my name the way I want to hear it."

Her next attempt was swallowed by a consuming kiss, and this time, when he tore his mouth from hers, she said it. It rushed forth as the endearment he longed for, demanded: *"Jared."* His reply rasped on the brink of another kiss: "I love you."

"IT'S ON PAUSE," Jared said. "If you hear anything, all you have to do is give this button a nudge."

"I can handle a tape recorder," Caroline replied.

Jared grabbed her hand and gave it a gentle yank, urging her into his arms. He exhaled a disconcerted sigh. "What am I doing leaving you alone in this house with a damned tape recorder?"

"You're going to a meeting of the Taggartville Chamber of Commerce Steering Committee," Caroline said crisply.

"I could skip it."

"You can't rat out on the committee. And would you quit worrying about me. We haven't heard a peep out of our ghosts all week. They may not show up again for another sixty or seventy years."

"You could come with me."

"No way. From what you've told me about how boring those committee meetings are, I'll take my chances on the ghosts."

"You wouldn't have to go to the meeting. You could just hang around the Cow Café."

"I don't feel like hanging around the Cow Café, Jared. It's been a lousy day, and I'm kind of looking forward to a quiet evening at home. I'm finally going to finish reading *Topper*."

"Let's just hope it turns out to be quiet," Jared said somberly. "And that the only ghosts you encounter are the ones between the covers of that book."

"If Katherine and Samuel should decide to go dancing again, I know what to expect. And I'll play the entire thing for you when you get home."

Jared looked dubious.

"I'll be okay," she said. "Now quit fretting over me like a Victorian papa and go to your meeting. The Taggartville Chamber of Commerce needs you."

Caroline heaved a sigh of relief when she heard Jared's car leaving. She couldn't deny feeling a little apprehension over being alone in the house again, but she was actually looking forward to a few hours to herself.

It had, as she'd told Jared, been a lousy day that started with a phone call informing her that one of the wallpaper patterns she'd selected had been discontinued. She'd spent the rest of the morning and much of the afternoon on the phone trying to find a warehouse or supplier with a back inventory. The weather wasn't helping much, either. It was overcast and cold—not freezing, but humid and cool enough to send a chill through the bones of anyone who'd become accustomed to mild temperatures and sunny days. So Caroline had been forced to dig out the sweatshirt, jeans and socks in which she'd started her trip south.

And if discontinued wallpaper and a miserable cold spell weren't vexing enough, Caroline had started her period, which always made her feel out of sorts. She dreaded the inevitable awkward moment when she had to share that tidbit of news with Jared.

Another milestone in a new love affair, Caroline thought. As she reflected on it, it was difficult to believe she'd known

Jared for such a short time; that just three weeks ago she'd been traveling south with Dessie, glad to be leaving the dreary Massachusetts winter behind and looking forward to the change of pace. She'd been enchanted by the idea of working on Katherine House.

Three weeks ago, Caroline hadn't anticipated that she'd actually *live* in Katherine House, that she'd encounter ghosts there, that she'd have an affair with Jared Colin. Falling in love hadn't been part of the plan, any more than having ghosts dancing above her head had been.

Three weeks, she thought, gratefully sinking onto her bed. She hugged a pillow and wondered morosely where she'd be in another three weeks. Jared had said he loved her, but they hadn't discussed the future—the possibilities or impossibilities, the probabilities or improbabilities of their personal relationship lasting after the last scrap of wallpaper or window curtain was hung in Katherine House. For all Caroline knew, Jared might love every woman he became intimate with.

Desdemona leaped onto the bed, stiffened momentarily to regain her balance, and mewed.

"Well, hello, stranger," Caroline said, reaching out to pet the cat. Dessie sidled up to her, plopped down, rolled on her back and purred while Caroline scratched her chest.

"We haven't had a lot of time like this together lately, have we, Dessie? You've been usurped as a bedfellow, haven't you?"

If Dessie held a grudge, she hid it well. After a few minutes of petting, snores replaced her purrs. Caroline shook her head at the almost comical snorts and whistles. "Crazy cat!"

She might have dozed; she'd never be certain whether she was actually asleep or simply tottering on the verge of sleep, when Dessie's low growl roused her to full wakefulness.

"What is it, girl?" Caroline asked, but she already knew. In all the years she'd owned Dessie, she'd heard her growl that way only a few times before, and always in this house. Muscles tensed in anticipation, Caroline rolled over and dropped her feet to the floor, then crossed the room and flipped on the tape recorder.

As if brought to life by the switch she'd just hit, music drifted down from above. *"Three O'Clock in the Morning."* Caroline went back to her bed and hugged a pillow to her chest, waiting for the laughter, the scuffling sounds of feet on the floor in waltz time. Eventually, as she knew it would, the music slowed and ceased, to be replaced by the sounds of heavy breathing and urgent, rhythmic scraping.

Caroline had thought she was prepared for it—forewarned and forearmed. But as she hugged the pillow tighter, she felt her heart pounding in her chest and the blood pulsing through her temples. The air she drew into her lungs with ragged effort seemed thin and oxygen poor. Her hands became claws, spasmodically clutching the pillow. A silent scream lodged in her dry throat as the scraping reached a fevered pace, and the sensual sighs and groans from above grew explicitly sexual.

Shrill cries of passion fulfilled were followed by a sudden, vacuous silence that seemed sacrosanct. Caroline took guarded breaths, not wanting to breach that horrid silence.

At last she became aware of the muffled scrape of the tape turning inside the tape recorder, and that mechanical scrape, so mundane and normal, was reassuring. The normalcy of it gave her the strength to move, and she got up and turned off the recorder, wishing she had the courage to rewind it and play it back to see if anything had been captured on tape. But she was almost afraid to know, and her fingers were shaking too much to manipulate the proper buttons, anyway.

She had just begun to relax, when a new sound came from above—a scream, piercing and terror-filled. The sounds that followed were even more horrible: pleas and hysterical denials. The grunts of human beings straining in a physical fight. The desperate thrashing of human beings involved in mortal combat. The guttural wheezing of a human being struggling for air.

Caroline stood frozen, listening to that terrible aural panorama of violence. If she could have turned on the recorder again, she would have, but she was paralyzed. Her hands and feet were heavy. Her arms hung limply at her side. And she felt as though someone had catapulted an anvil onto her chest.

The phone rang. Caroline jumped, inhaling raggedly in shock. Whatever had been going on in the Kaleidoscope Room ceased abruptly, leaving in its wake a dreadful silence that was almost palpable—a silence that smelled strongly of lavender.

An eternity passed before the phone rang a second time. Caroline jerked the receiver from the hook and lifted it to her ear, but was too distraught to speak into the mouthpiece.

"Caroline?" Jared's voice was anxious.

"It smells like lavender," Caroline said distractedly.

"I'll be right there."

She was still standing next to the bed, holding the phone against her ear, when Jared sprinted up the stairs eight minutes later.

He pried the phone from her fingers and replaced it, then pulled Caroline against his chest. With a shuddering sigh, she wrapped her arms around his waist and collapsed against him, turning from stone to jelly as she clung to him.

Jared chastised himself for leaving her when every instinct he possessed had been telling him not to. He held her for several minutes before asking, "Want to tell me about it?"

"The same as before," she said. "Only . . . more. Worse."

"Did you get it on tape?"

"The recorder was running," she said. "I haven't checked." *I'm afraid to check, afraid of finding nothing there.*

"Do you feel steady enough for me to check it out?"

Caroline lifted her head from his chest and nodded. She sank onto the edge of the bed and watched him work with the recorder. Finally, he hit Play. At first there was just the muted scrape of blank tape, and Caroline held her breath, hoping against hope that the entire tape wasn't blank. Then came the familiar waltz, scratchy but readily recognizable. Relief sapped Caroline's strength and heat rose from her chest, to her neck and face.

Listening intently, Jared paled, then absently thrust his fingers through his hair, then wrung his hands over his face. He wasn't sure what he'd been expecting, something more ethereal or mysterious, perhaps. He certainly hadn't expected it to sound so ordinary, so...human, or so...explicit. He experienced a sense of déjà vu, the same instant recognition of the parallel between what he was hearing and the time he'd spent in the Kaleidoscope Room with Caroline, listening to the same song; laughing, dancing, kissing.

The emotions were the same, she'd said, and now he understood what she'd meant. As the erotic shuffling of a passionate encounter replaced the waltz, he turned to look at Caroline. She was curled up on the bed, eyes closed, wrapping a pillow around her head, holding the edges against her ears to block out the recording.

Jared listened until the tape went blank, then sat down next to Caroline and gently pushed her hands away from the pillow.

"Do you believe me now?" she asked softly.

His eyes met hers with reassurance. "I never doubted you."

"There was more this time. I had just turned off the recorder when I heard a scream, and—" She threw her arms around his neck. "Oh, Jared, I think he was killing her."

"Samuel would never have hurt Katherine."

"Maybe it wasn't Samuel."

"No," Jared said. "Katherine was devoted to Samuel. She wouldn't have—"

Caroline pulled away so that she could see his face. "How can you be so sure?"

"Because of the things my grandfather told me about her."

"She was his older sister. He idolized her. He may not have been objective."

"Maybe it isn't Katherine and Samuel up there," he suggested. "It could be a different couple altogether."

Caroline considered the prospect. "It was Katherine's Victrola, Jared. Her house, her record, her perfume."

"Katherine couldn't have been murdered in the cupola when she died a hundred miles from here. Her death is well documented."

"And ghosts haunt the place of death."

"Maybe not all ghosts read the rule book!" Jared objected, his frustration showing. "Damn! None of this makes any sense."

"Ghosts don't have to make sense," Caroline pointed out.

Jared gave a self-derisive snort. "Listen to us. We're talking about ghosts the way we would discuss something on the evening news."

"I wish I'd gone upstairs," Caroline said. "I might have seen . . . something. But I was paralyzed."

"Let's go up now," Jared suggested.

"Last time, when the cops were here, there was no sign of anything," Caroline said. "But this time, there was a struggle. Maybe—"

But the Kaleidoscope Room was in order—the stylus on the Victrola still folded back, the records perfectly arranged in the drawer, everything else equally undisturbed.

Jared stood in the middle of the room and did a slow survey of it from floor to cupola dome, wall to wall and window to window. "How could anything make so much racket and not even stir a speck of dust?" Jared asked.

Caroline merely shook her head. She had no answers for him—only feelings, impressions, intuition.

As though he felt compelled to exhaust every lead, Jared made a cursory examination of the room, searching, as Caroline had searched a week previously, for wires or speakers; searching, as she had searched, for evidence that there was a tangible, rationally acceptable explanation for the phenomena captured on tape.

Finding no more than she had found, he turned to Caroline for comfort, stretching his arm across her shoulders and taking reassurance from having her so close. "Let's take a walk, get out of this house for a while."

They didn't go far, just a couple of blocks up the road and back, walking briskly to combat the cold that nipped at their noses and ears and turned their breath to steam.

"Do you want to leave Katherine House?" Jared asked.

Caroline gave him a sideways glance. "Trying to kick me out again?"

Jared refused to be distracted by her touch of levity. "There's no reason for you to have to put up with any of this. We'll find a room—an apartment for you—somewhere."

"What about you?"

"Katherine House belongs to me."

"So you're staying."

"I don't scare off so easily."

"But you think I should?"

"The ghosts, if that's what they are, are my problem, not yours."

Caroline stopped abruptly. "I'm the one they perform for. It seems to me that makes them my problem as much as yours."

The night was overcast, and fog suffused the beam from the nearest streetlamp into a hazy halo. Caroline's face was a pale oval in the darkness, framed by blond hair that captured the faint light in the curves of its waves. Jared lifted his fingertips to her cheek, and was surprised at how cool it was.

Caroline tilted her head back to look him fully in the face. Even in the dimness, Jared could see the vulnerability in her eyes. "Do you want me to leave?" she asked softly.

"No. But I don't want you upset, or hurt, either."

"I don't want to wimp out!" she said, with surprising force.

"If anything happened to you—"

"You've given me the option of leaving. If I choose to stay, you won't have to feel responsible."

"It's not that simple, Caroline. I do feel responsible for you."

"This is one of those protective male-macho things, isn't it?" she asked, putting her hands on his shoulders.

"This is a man in love with a woman and concerned about her safety."

"Jared."

"You know I hate it when you say my name that way. Hey, what's this?" The sleeves of her sweatshirt were pulled down, covering her hands. "You're cold, aren't you?"

Taking her sleeved hands in his own, he guided them around his waist, inside his parka. "Why didn't you say something?"

"It's not all that cold," she replied. "I'm just used to wearing gloves, and I didn't bring mine."

"Let's go home," he said, draping his arm across her shoulders to warm her as they walked. Back at the house, they made hot chocolate and carried it into Jared's den and drank it while Jared caught the end of the evening news.

"I'm going to the library tomorrow," Caroline said, during the commercials between the weather and the sports. "I think it's time we checked out the Tragic Derailment of 1930."

"You truly believe Katherine died in this house, don't you?"

"I heard her die in this house tonight."

Jared hit the remote control to turn off the TV and opened his arms to her in invitation. Caroline put down her mug and curled up next to him, accepting his comfort. "You can watch the sports, Jared. I'm okay."

Caroline grinned when he immediately turned the television back on. She really didn't mind, though. Let him concentrate on sports; for the moment, the solidity and warmth of his body were reassuring enough.

She was almost asleep in the blissful comfort of his arms when Jared kissed her temple, and then her cheek, and she realized that he'd turned the television off.

He was kissing her before she could stop him, and when he raised his mouth from hers, he whispered, "Let's go to bed."

Caroline swallowed hesitantly. "We need to talk about that."

He studied her face questioningly.

"I'm out of commission for a few days," she said. "The . . . uh, female thing. I just wouldn't be comfortable—"

"Do you think sex is the only reason I want you near me?"

"You wouldn't mind just holding me?"

"Mind? I love having you next to me." *Knowing you're mine.* "I'm not the insensitive bastard you think I am." *And I'm getting a little tired of having to tell you that.*

"I didn't mean to imply that you were insensitive. I just thought I should warn you before we had any . . . awkward surprises."

"After the scare you got tonight from our resident ghosts and the scare I got calling you and having you sound like a zombie over the phone, a good night's sleep will probably do us both good."

"Umm," Caroline responded wistfully, snuggling against his chest.

"We probably wouldn't be in the mood, even if circumstances were different."

"Speak for yourself," she said with a sigh. At the moment, she wouldn't be adverse to a dose of oblivion.

"I just said that to make you feel better. You know I'm always in the mood with you, Sugar Lips."

"Silver-tongued devil," Caroline teased, but it crossed her mind that Jared had done a lot of white lying for her benefit. Like the instant story he'd made up for Mrs. Kippirich. Apparently truth, to Jared Colin, was a flexible commodity. "You're right, though. A good night's sleep will probably do us both some good."

But it was not to be a blissful night's sleep. Jared woke Caroline, thrashing about and calling out the same plaintive cries as before: "Cat. Oh, God. No, Cat."

Caroline shook him awake. He stared at her with blank, wild eyes for a moment, then lay back in the bed, pulling her with him, clinging to her urgently.

"You were dreaming again," she said. "Do you remember any of it?"

His chest heaved with his hard breathing. "No. There's just this feeling of . . . terror."

"You were calling out for someone named Cat."

"Katherine?"

"You've had the dream twice, and both times, it's been after we've had a . . . *manifestation*."

Jared took a long time answering. "Is that what's going on? We're having manifestations?"

"It's as good a word as any."

Again, Jared took a long time replying. "I never met her, but she—and her story—were a part of my life, the way a favorite book or a favorite song is part of your life. It's not easy for me to accept that that part of my life could be a lie."

"Legends are seldom what they seem."

"She was more than a legend. She was family. She was my grandfather's sister."

"Even if things didn't happen the way they've been recorded, there's a chance we'll never find out what really happened," Caroline said.

"I don't know whether to hope we do, or hope we don't."

Though she couldn't see his face in the darkness, Caroline heard the vulnerability in his words. After a long pause, she asked, "Do you think Taggart used the same shaving soap as our grandfathers?"

"I don't know. Why?"

"Because I smelled it tonight in the Kaleidoscope Room. Mixed in with the lavender."

"I was wearing it."

"You have a light touch with it. I only notice it when I'm close to you. You were across the room from me when I smelled it upstairs."

Jared thought about it awhile. "Katherine gave my grandfather his first cake of that soap in a porcelain shaving mug the year he learned to shave. Taggart might have worn it. It could have been her favorite because of that."

But Taggart didn't die in the Kaleidoscope Room, Caroline thought, but decided to keep that to herself. Jared was distressed enough over the possibility that Katherine might not have died the way he'd always believed.

"Caroline?" he whispered.

"Umm?"

"You asked if I'd mind just holding you tonight."

"Uh-hmm."

"I'm not so sure who's holding whom now."

"Does it matter?"

"It matters that you're here," he said, hugging her tighter. "That matters."

IN 1930 *THE TAGGARTVILLE News Journal* was a semiweekly. Caroline started her research with the first issue following the date of Katherine's death. *Alleged date,* she thought dourly. It had taken her several days to get up the courage to come to the library after the harrowing experience with the ghosts, especially with Jared so insistent that she was wrong about the theory that Katherine had not died on the train, as everyone believed.

The Tragic Derailment story had been given the front-page, banner-headline treatment to be expected in a semiweekly newspaper in a small town in 1930 when a prominent citizen had been killed in a catastrophe that, in itself, would have merited the banner heads.

24 BODIES IDENTIFIED, 103 INJURED, OVER 40 MISSING IN TRAGIC TRAIN DERAILMENT
KATHERINE TAGGART, WIFE OF SAMUEL TAGGART, BELIEVED AMONG THE DEAD

There was a picture of Katherine—a formal portrait in which her hair was piled atop her head and she was wearing a white dress with a high, lace-trimmed collar.

Genetics, Caroline thought, as she looked at the grainy photo. There, two generations removed, were Jared's fair skin, his dark hair, and a feminine rendering of his exquisite bone structure. There was something of Jared's mouth in that mouth, a trace of his cocky attitude in the daring tilt of her chin.

The familiar newspaper format of headlines, text, photos and captions lent the account of the accident a sense of immediacy. Despite the florid language, Caroline was drawn into the drama and tragedy of the derailment, and she shivered as she read the quotes of eyewitnesses describing the anguished screams of victims, fires that lit up the dark of the night, and "sights too ghastly for the human eye to behold."

Katherine Taggart, wife of prominent Taggartville businessman and philanthropist Samuel Taggart, is missing and believed to be among those dead but not yet identified. Mrs. Taggart boarded the westbound train at the Orlando station, late in the afternoon on the day of the derailment. She was en route to Tallahassee to attend the graduation ceremonies at Florida State University, where her brother, Mitchell Colin, son of Myra Colin, owner of Colin's Breads, was to receive his diploma.

On the day of Mrs. Taggart's departure, Mr. and Mrs. Taggart had been shopping in Orlando, and it was decided that by boarding the train in Orlando, Mrs. Taggart might secure more advantageous seating than if she returned to Taggartville and boarded at the local station, which is three stops farther down the line.

Identification of the bodies has been hampered by the conditions of many of the victims due to fire and battering within the cars as the train flew from the tracks and rolled down an embankment. Also complicating the identification process is the fact that the car in which 21 members of the Young Women's Christian Choir were traveling was among those that caught fire, and many of the young women were nearly the same size and age as Mrs. Taggart.

Already, they were referring to the accident as the Tragic

Derailment of 1930. Sitting in the library more than six decades later, reading the accounts on the monitor of a microfilm reading device, Caroline understood why. Her heart went out to Jared, who'd probably never fully realized the scope of the horror of the accident that, according to legend, had taken his great-aunt's life.

Poor Samuel Taggart. If Katherine had been, in fact, aboard that train, how awful it must have been for him to read about mangled steel and anguished screams and charred bodies. What must it have been like to be a member of one of those victims' families, and to have to wait for the tedious process of identification?

She photocopied the relevant stories before reeling ahead to the next issue. There was an update of the accident statistics, and another photo of Katherine, alongside the headline: "Katherine Taggart's Death Confirmed. Wedding Ring is Key to Identification."

The next issue included a florid account of Katherine's funeral, from the "room filled with sympathy wreaths and sprays of spring flowers" to the "blanket of roses that draped the closed coffin of a woman whose beauty would have surpassed that of any blossom which graced the velvet-lined receptacle."

Caroline buried her face in her hands and sighed. What she'd learned both confirmed the possibility that her suspicions could be correct, and made the idea that Katherine Taggart had died anywhere but on that ill-fated train seem ludicrous. A ring slipped on the finger of a charred corpse— Would Samuel Taggart have been capable of such a macabre act of deception to conceal a murder and avoid scandal?

She photocopied the account of Katherine's funeral, but not before noticing another story related to the accident.

LOCAL MAN FEARED VICTIM OF TRAGIC DE-
RAILMENT

Fear continues to mount that Taggartville resident Sven Yorick was among those yet unidentified victims of the Tragic Derailment. Concern that Yorick might have been aboard the wrecked train was sparked when he failed to report to work at the Taggartville Ice Company on the Tuesday following the tragedy. Mr. Charles Dyce, owner of the Taggartville Ice Company, says that Yorick, familiar to many Taggartville citizens through his ice delivery route, was a reliable worker who would not have intentionally missed work.

A search of Mr. Yorick's rooms at the boardinghouse on the corner of Orange and Oak streets revealed that a suitcase and some personal items were missing, leading to speculation that Mr. Yorick might have boarded the westbound train. A physical description of Mr. Yorick has been forwarded to authorities in charge of identifying victims of the rail accident.

Crediting curiosity as much as intuition, Caroline copied that story, too, before scrolling to the next issue, where she found an update on how many bodies had been found, how many identified, and how many of the wounded had died since the last death tally. She copied it primarily for the last paragraph.

Due to the impossibility of making positive identification of many of the victims, a plan has been proposed for a special cemetery for the unidentified victims near the site of the accident. Under the plan, individual graves would be marked with a cross or Star of David, and the names of the victims would be inscribed on a central monument. Mr. Mark Somma, owner of the property on either side of the derailment site, has offered to donate an acre of land to be dedicated to the cemetery and memorial.

The stories grew progressively shorter and increasingly repetitive in the next issues. Convinced that she had gleaned all the information she was going to glean about the Tragic Derailment of 1930, Caroline rewound the microfilm and re-placed it in the files.

She exited the library with a sense of relief. The sun was shining brightly, tempering the cold and burning off the gloom of the previous evening, and suddenly ghosts and bloody, smoldering derailed trains seemed distant realities. Caroline fed the parking meter coins until she had accrued credit for the maximum time allowable and set off for the Cow Café, where she was to meet Jared for lunch.

She was early, but Jared had beaten her there and claimed his customary table near the window. The waitress was at the table with a pitcher of iced tea before Caroline was settled into the chair properly.

"You two want the special?"

Jared looked at Caroline, who nodded, and then at the waitress. "Two specials it is, Betty."

He turned back to Caroline when Betty hurried off to an-other table on her way to the order window. "So, how'd it go at the library? Find out anything?"

"More than I ever wanted to know about the Tragic De-railment," Caroline replied. "You're not going to like it."

Jared visibly steeled himself for unpleasant news. "Let's hear it."

"It'll wait until after lunch," she said, and when he poised his mouth to protest, squelched him with, "Believe me, you'll thank me for waiting."

"So," he said, "aside from the ghosts in the attic and the bad news at the library, how is life treating you?"

Caroline didn't have a chance to answer before a young man approached the table tentatively. "Mr. Colin? I'm Jeff Adams from the *Journal*. I wrote the piece about your plans to renovate Katherine House."

"Of course," Jared replied, extending his hand to Jeff. "You'll be interested in meeting Caroline Naylor. She's the decorator who's taking the idea from concept to reality."

"Good to meet you," Jeff said, taking Caroline's right hand when she offered it. Everything from his tone of voice to the delighted gleam in his eye underscored how good it was.

Jared stopped just short of clearing his throat to regain the reporter's attention. Caroline couldn't pinpoint the body language he used to imply possession to the young man, but it was apparent that he had sent a message—*Don't even consider it*—to Jeff Adams, and that Jeff Adams had received that message, loud and clear.

Jared's possessiveness both irritated and flattered her; it even provoked a grudging respect for his skill at unspoken male communication.

Adams was all business as he turned back to Jared. "There're some rumors flying around about trouble at Katherine House."

"Trouble?" Jared asked.

"Something about prowlers, and a phone call that had you shooting out of here faster than a hunter who's bumped into a skunk."

An awkward, extended pause followed before Adams prompted, "Well, is there a story here, or not?"

"Don't stop the presses, Adams," Jared said, adopting a chummy, good-old-boy tone. "We had some mice in the cupola."

"Mice?" Adams repeated.

"Pesky little devils. Make a hell of a noise."

"And I'm supposed to believe that you tore out of a meeting because there were mice running around in your attic."

"Cupola," Jared corrected. "Hell, Adams, you know how gossip gets blown out of proportion. The truth is, Caroline here isn't too fond of mice, and—" he winked broadly "—I like playing hero."

The set of Jeff Adams's jaw bespoke residual skepticism.

"Ask the cops who answered the call the other night. It shouldn't be difficult to find out who was on duty."

Adams looked like a child whose balloon had just popped. With a good-natured shrug of his shoulders, he said, "Guess it was just a false lead."

Jared tilted his head and gave a sympathetic lift of his eyebrows. "Sorry—no crime waves at Katherine House."

"Don't forget to call if anything should crop up," Adams said.

"I've got your number in my card file next to the phone," Jared assured him. "Nice seeing you, Jeff."

As the reporter moved away, Caroline kept telling herself she didn't really want to throttle Jared—at least not in public, in front of the Cow Café lunch crowd and the boy reporter. "Thanks a lot!" she said. "The cops were convinced I was a hysterical female last week. Now you've as much as told it to the press."

"Was I supposed to tell him about Katherine Taggart's ghost's 'sensual escapades' in the Kaleidoscope Room?"

Caroline glared at him a moment before saying, "You live in a fishbowl, Jared."

"It's a small town."

"And you're a celebrity."

"And Katherine House is a landmark, and you're a beautiful stranger, all of which makes us targets for observation, speculation and gossip in a town like Taggartville."

Caroline paused thoughtfully. "If you go into politics, you'll always live in a fishbowl."

Jared shrugged. "I'll just have to keep my act clean."

"And finesse your way out of awkward situations. You're very good at finessing, Jared."

Jared answered with a cocky grin, and once again, Caroline found his ability to bend truth conveniently and with such ease both admirable and disconcerting. No doubt about it, he was a good man to have on your side in a crisis. But what about when there wasn't a crisis? Was he a man who could be trusted? Or was he at his best when he was at his worst?

Caroline wasn't sure, and she tried not to think about it as she ate her lunch.

BY THE TIME CAROLINE returned to her car and drove back to Katherine House, Jared was already there, seated behind his desk and sorting the day's mail.

She hesitated in the doorway of his office, still reluctant to reopen the Pandora's box the newspaper articles had opened at the library.

"You got some mail," Jared said, tapping a stack of three envelopes he'd put near the front edge of the desk.

Caroline sat down in the chair facing his desk and picked them up, then flipped through them. None was urgent.

"So," Jared began, "what is it I'm not going to like?"

Caroline summarized the articles for him. "So you see, it wasn't as simple as Katherine being killed and her body being shipped home. With the victims burned so badly, there's room for doubt."

The expression on Jared's face turned grim. He wasn't ready to have his illusions shattered, his foundations shaken. And he didn't like her for threatening to do the shattering and shaking.

"Don't shoot the messenger," Caroline pleaded. "I didn't make up the facts—I found them on microfilm at the public library."

"Katherine was on that train, going to my grandfather's graduation ceremonies."

"Her coffin was closed, Jared. The only way her body was identified was by a ring. At least admit that there's room for doubt."

"Caroline—"

"You don't really believe that I heard her, do you, Jared?"

"Of course, I do. I heard the tapes."

"Not the parts that would have cast doubt on what you've always believed about Katherine. And because you haven't heard them—"

She stopped abruptly. Jared watched the color drain from her face. "Caroline?"

"You weren't supposed to hear," she said. Her eyes met his. "Don't you see? She waits until you're out of the house."

"Damn it, Caroline!" He punctuated the exclamation with a pound of his fist on his desk. "Do you think ghosts have brains? These ghosts—if that's what they are—don't even have substance. How could they think?"

"Ghosts have been known to suddenly appear to warn loved ones about deadly threats, to save them from catastrophe. Maybe it's not so much thinking as feeling."

"If Katherine is showing herself suddenly, why would she show herself to you and not to me? What possible logic is there in that? She's *my* relative, not yours!"

Caroline tilted her head at a curious angle. "Is this an ego thing, Jared? Does it offend you that she'd choose me over you?"

"Don't be absurd."

Absurd? His attitude rankled Caroline. "It's not absurd. Maybe she doesn't think the same way we do. Maybe she senses things. Maybe she sensed that I could be objective, and you weren't ready to learn the truth. Maybe she knew I'd be receptive, and you'd resist what she's trying to tell us. Maybe she's protecting you."

"From what?"

"From the truth!"

"Which is?"

"Possibly, that she didn't die in that train. That she and Samuel didn't have the perfect storybook marriage. That she was a human being instead of a legend. Maybe she's tired, Jared. Maybe being a legend has worn her out."

Jared released a long, anguished sigh. "Listen to us, Caroline. We're arguing—we're having a goddammed *philosophical* argument—about ghosts!"

His eyes, as he lifted his gaze to hers, were the eyes of a man haunted—not by ghosts, but by his own doubts and fears and uncertainties. "I love you, Caroline." He said it as though it should forestall all problems, solve all riddles. "Let's not argue over questions that have no answers."

Caroline met his gaze evenly. "The other side of that desk seems a long way away."

"It's not so far," he said, a smile of relief sliding onto his face as he rose and crossed the not-so-distant distance.

He kissed her, gently, thoroughly, and still holding her, said, "We'll get to the bottom of this."

A knock at the door startled them. They jumped, then looked at each other and laughed at their own skittishness. "That's probably Aunt Essie," Caroline said. "I told her I'd show her the wallpaper patterns I picked out."

"Talk about coming back to reality."

Aunt Essie was indeed a virtual paragon of reality as she marched in in her sensible thick-soled, leather lace-ups, with her blue-gray bun bouncing precariously on top of her head, anchored with silver hairpins perpetually on the brink of sliding out. Her inevitable print dress was the final touch that made Aunt Essie a dose of reassuring predictability in the face of the extraordinary events of the past two weeks.

"Hope I'm not interrupting anything," she said.

"Now, Aunt Essie," Jared teased, "what could you possibly be interrupting?"

Aunt Essie chuckled. "I'm not so old that I've forgotten what it's like for young people."

"We were just opening the mail," Jared said innocently.

Aunt Essie cocked an eyebrow and cast him a sharp-eyed look. "We played post office in my day, too."

In the overall scheme of things, Caroline thought wryly, *some things change constantly, and others never change at all.* Aunt Essie was one of the constants. At that moment she reminded Caroline so much of her grandmother that Caroline almost threw her arms around her.

"Aunt Essie!" Jared said. "I'm shocked at you."

Aunt Essie fixed another of her shrewd-bird looks on Jared. "Don't you play innocent with me, mister. It's all over town that you two are a 'hot item.' In my day, we'd have said you were 'spooning.'"

Jared winked at Caroline. "Our secret's out!"

"Ha!" Aunt Essie cackled triumphantly.

"I'm not confessing to anything!" Caroline said. "Except to making some brilliant decisions regarding wallpaper. Let's go take a look."

Carrying her sketches and the wallpaper samples, she led Aunt Essie from room to room on the second floor, explaining in detail what she had planned for each. "We're calling this the Garden Room," she said, in the room with the tall windows. She showed her the wallpaper she'd selected, which had an ecru background with pale green stripes and a muted leaf motif in even paler green. "We'll fill the corner with hanging baskets and potted plants, of course, and set up the brass bed."

Aunt Essie nodded approval. "I told Jared you'd be perfect for this job."

Caroline smiled. "This job has been a dream assignment." *Complete with fairy-tale and nightmare aspects.*

Aunt Essie put her withered hand on Caroline's and whispered confidentially, "He's in love with you. I can tell from the way he looks at you."

Caroline felt her face coloring and turned her head away from Aunt Essie's sharp eyes. "You're a hopeless romantic, Aunt Essie."

"The way he looks at you," Aunt Essie persisted, and sighed dramatically. "It still makes my heart swell to see a man look at a woman that way. My Thomas used to look at me like that." She chortled, mocking her own sentimentality. "Fifty-five years ago, my Thomas looked at me that way. A month later, he married me."

"Things were simpler then," Caroline said.

Aunt Essie smiled indulgently, rather like an overbearingly patient kindergarten teacher. "There are things that never change. Love is one of them. It has never been simple, my dear."

Caroline chose not to debate the point with her. Instead, she led the way into the master suite, where Desdemona greeted them with an indignant meow, then proceeded to weave in and out around Caroline's legs as she walked.

"Dessie!" Caroline scolded, then shot Aunt Essie a wry look. "My cat, Desdemona."

"You never know what a cat will do," Aunt Essie said. "They're all high-strung."

"She's been a little strange ever since we moved in," Caroline explained.

"She's a handsome animal. Nice coat."

"Thank you," Caroline said, then reverted to business. "I thought dusty rose should be the dominant color in here, with pale green accents. Here's the wallpaper pattern."

Aunt Essie examined the floral print and nodded approval. "That tester bed demands a Victorian touch."

"I thought so, too. This was Katherine and Samuel's room. I want it to be special."

"It will be, Cookie," Aunt Essie said, nodding absently. "It will be."

They stood there a few minutes, just looking around the room, with its high ceiling, striped walls and fussy wainscoting. "The workmanship," Aunt Essie murmured. "It's such a shame we're losing all the fine workmanship. If we don't preserve it, it could be lost forever." She turned her gaze to Caroline's face. "We need more conscientious people like Jared Colin."

"This house holds great sentimental value for Jared because his grandfather left it to him. He's lucky he can afford to renovate and maintain it. Not everyone can."

"We're *all* lucky he can afford to renovate and maintain it," Aunt Essie said gravely. "People these days would just as soon tear down an old house with character and put up a ticky-tacky box with central air and heat. Somebody's got to save a bit of it along the way."

Caroline smiled. "That's why we have you and the society."

Aunt Essie shrugged. "We do what we can, but it's like trying to fill an ocean with an eyedropper."

A silence followed. Finally Caroline said, "Jared asked me to help put together a pamphlet about Katherine Taggart. I've been reading about the Tragic Derailment. I know you would have been very young, but do you remember it at all?"

"Oh, of course. It was the biggest story since the hurricane of '26. Of course, we didn't have television back then, so we didn't *see* it on film at eleven. But it was awful enough. Everyone talked about what a shame it was that something that terrible could happen to a woman like Katherine Taggart. She was quite beautiful."

"I was surprised to read that there might have been another victim from Taggartville. Sven Yorick, the ice man."

"Well, now, they were never sure about him. There was talk at the time." Aunt Essie sniffed. "I was only a child, you understand, so I only heard what I could manage to overhear. People didn't talk much in front of children then."

"What did they say about him?"

"The man was a rounder. Handsome as the very devil. Scandinavian, you see. Talked with an accent. Mother always tried to scurry us off somewhere when she saw him coming, but my sister and I— My sister was two years older than I. She passed on, it would be, oh, eighteen years ago this coming April— My sister and I always managed to sneak a peep at him when he delivered the ice. He was big as a mountain, and had curly strawberry-blond hair and ruddy cheeks. We thought he was a Viking."

"Why didn't your mother want you seeing him?"

Aunt Essie cackled. "Why, it just wasn't proper. Young girls weren't supposed to be so . . . stimulated back then." She laughed again. "But we saw him. Lordy, but he had broad shoulders! And those eyes—blue as deep water."

"What did they say about his disappearance?"

"The talk was that he'd been planning to run off with a married woman. He'd told some friends of his down at the beer joint he'd been seeing someone and was going to leave with her."

She cackled again. "There was more than one husband worried, believe you me! The milkman stopped on the doorstep, but the ice man actually came into the kitchen, and a woman would have had to be blindfolded not to notice a man like Sven Yorick!"

"So when he disappeared, they thought he'd run off with someone's wife?"

"Yep! And there was more than one sigh of relief that it wasn't any wife from Taggartville."

"Did they ever find out if he was on the train?"

"Oh, there was some ruckus over putting his name on that monument, but if he ever got on that train, he didn't get on in Taggartville. Folks figured maybe he had a woman in one of the outlying areas and caught the train farther down the line. Or he just took off, and it was pure coincidence, that train derailing like it did."

"Did they put his name on the monument?"

"No. Nobody saw him get on the train, and they didn't have any bodies that fit his description. If they'd had his body, they'd have known it. There weren't that many men who grew to six-foot-six back then."

"Six-foot-six?" Caroline mused.

"I told you!" Aunt Essie said. "The man was big as a mountain. This day and age, a man with his looks would wind up dancing for the Chippendales or playing the hunk on a soap opera."

"Aunt Essie!" Caroline teased. "What do you know about the Chippendales?"

Aunt Essie snorted indignantly. "Went to see them, that's what I know. Two years ago when they were in Orlando. A body's got to keep current, you know. Took my eldest great-granddaughter." She exhaled what might have been a sigh. "Nice-looking bunch of boys, although most of them could have used a haircut. One of them reminded me of my eldest grandson. He was something of a beach boy back in the sixties."

This time Caroline did give in to the urge to hug the older woman. "Aunt Essie, you're priceless!"

"What's this?"

Both women turned, surprised by Jared's presence.

"Aunt Essie was just telling me how she went to see the Chippendale dancers," Caroline replied.

"Funny you should mention dancers," Jared said. "Aunt Essie, did Caroline show you the Victrola?"

"Did you get it back already?" Aunt Essie asked.

"All it needed was a good cleaning. Why don't we go up and give it a spin?"

Jared was a study in gallantry as he braced Aunt Essie's elbow and assisted her up the stairs. He went over to the Victrola and wound it, then opened the drawer and rummaged through the records. "We found a lovely waltz. Ah, here it is!"

He held up one of the discs. Caroline recognized the label, and shot him a curious look. He returned a look that said, "Trust me," then put the record on the turntable.

"It's called—"

"'Three O'Clock in the Morning,'" Aunt Essie finished, as the melody swept through the room. "I know the song well. The orchestras used to play it as the last song of the evening." She closed her eyes and hummed, and a beatific expression claimed her face as she remembered dances from her youth.

Jared bowed in front of her. "May I have this dance?"

Aunt Essie's eyes flew open. "Me? Dance? Why, I haven't danced since my youngest daughter's wedding. The music these days—"

"Surely you remember how to waltz?" Jared cajoled, using his lady-killer grin to advantage. "It's like riding a bicycle. You never forget it."

"Oh, you!" Aunt Essie exclaimed, but she didn't protest when he put his arms around her and twirled her out into the middle of the room in a flawless waltz step.

Watching them, Caroline wondered what Jared was up to. She knew him well enough to know that there was usually method behind what seemed his momentary madness. The first notes of the waltz had prickled her scalp, and she'd tensed all over, but now she forced herself to relax by taking a deep breath and consciously uncoiling her hands, which she had unconsciously balled into fists.

There were no ghosts in the room now. It was just a lovely old room in a lovely old house, and Jared was dancing with a perfectly lovely old lady to a lovely old song.

The song ended, and Jared took his arms from around Aunt Essie.

"My!" she said. "I'd almost forgotten."

"Don't be so modest, Aunt Essie. You know you haven't forgotten anything since before World War II," Jared teased. He walked to the Victrola and lifted the stylus. Then, his eyes warm on Caroline's face, he said, "We really shouldn't leave the machine wound up."

The next thing Caroline knew, she was waltzing. "What are you up to?" she whispered.

"Extending an invitation," he said enigmatically.

"An invitation?"

"Shh. You'll spoil the mood." She might have protested, but he pulled her closer and whispered, "I'll explain later."

After Aunt Essie left, he insisted she accompany him to the little park on the lake just outside Taggartville. And there, while seated on a concrete bench shaded by the broad limbs of an oak tree, he explained what he had in mind.

After a long silence, he asked, "Well, what do you think?"

"I think," Caroline said, "that you are the only person I know who'd be presumptuous enough to try to outwit a ghost."

"But, do you think it'll work?"

Caroline shook her head in exasperation. "Of course, it'll work. When Jared Colin sets his mind to a task, even ghosts are outclassed. I just hope you don't break your bloody neck!"

12

"YOU KNOW WHAT TO DO?"

Caroline nodded. "We've gone over it at least a dozen times, Jared."

Jared dropped a brief kiss on her lips. "Then I'll see you later."

Caroline returned his wave as he drove off, then moved toward the house. *Maniac!* she thought, then paused before stepping onto the veranda to clear her mind of negative thoughts. She didn't know how perceptive ghosts were, but she didn't want to jinx Jared's plans by giving them away.

Humming some Beethoven, she forced herself to concentrate on the complicated melody, until, finally, she worked up the nerve to enter the house. She went directly upstairs, slipped off her shoes and, plumping the pillows against the headboard of her bed, settled down to finish reading Katherine Taggart's favorite book. Dessie, after demanding and receiving her quota of attention, curled up next to Caroline for a nap.

Caroline was in the middle of the final chapter by the time Dessie jerked away and began growling. The cat's back was arched and her fur was standing on end. Caroline patted her head. "Thanks for the warning, Dessie."

Then, reciting nursery rhymes in her head to keep from thinking of Jared, she reached for the switch of the lamp on the bedside table.

High diddle diddle/The cat and the fiddle—

She turned the light off, on, off, on.

The cow jumped over the moon—

Off. On. Inhaling sharply, Caroline lay back on the bed, waiting.

The little dog laughed/to see such a sight—

From the Kaleidoscope Room, the music began—the waltz.

And the dish ran away with the spoon.

Laughter came from above. Caroline leaped from the bed and switched on the tape recorder, then looked through the window—the window that had deliberately been left wide open, according to Jared's plan. From the limb of the magnolia tree that grew next to the house, the mastermind flashed her a cocky grin and a thumbs-up sign.

Caroline exhaled wearily. So far, so good. Above her, a couple waltzed to the plaintive music.

The Victrola wound down, the music ended. Caroline steeled herself for what came next. She yearned to look at Jared, take solace in his company, but she dared not.

Humpty Dumpty sat on a wall./ Humpty Dumpty had a great fall—

Caroline sighed. And in the Kaleidoscope Room, the ghosts made passionate love. Her cheeks colored; she knew Jared was watching her, although she couldn't watch him. He was a gate-crasher at this party.

From the cupola, the sighs and moans escalated to an ecstatic crescendo—the concert of lovers reaching sexual fulfillment.

In the silence that followed, Caroline held her breath, dreading what would come next. First there was the muted conversation—unintelligible murmuring of human voices being sifted through wood.

"Stop! No. When, don't . . ." The desperation in the plea sent shivers up Caroline's spine.

Then came the shuffling and thumping and grunting of mortal struggle.

And all the king's horses and all the king's men— Caroline thought intensely, clinging for a toehold on sanity.

A loud thunk, quite unghostly, caught her attention. She looked toward the source. "Jared?"

He pressed his fingers to his lips and pointed to the tape recorder.

"But—" she said, and then fell silent, caught up in the tense drama of watching Jared totter on the brink of disaster. He'd lifted the ladder he'd used to get to the tree and spread it from the limb to the windowsill, and he was crawling across it, with only the roof of the veranda to break his fall if he toppled off.

"The screen," he mouthed, pointing.

Caroline gave the screen a shove and it slid down the sloped roof of the veranda to land in the lower limbs of the tree. "You're a madman," she whispered as Jared crawled through the window, looking as relieved to be off the ladder as she was to see him off it.

He opened his arms and she ran to him, and they held each other, listening with rapt concentration while the scuffling ended abruptly, and then came the horrid choking sound of a human being gasping for air.

Jared spun away from Caroline and dashed for the door, and the stairway. She followed, calling his name.

He looked back briefly, with an expression that told her he wouldn't be stopped by anyone or anything short of death itself. The morbid image made her shiver, but she followed.

As he stepped onto the stairway, a man's anguished voice cried out, "No. Cat. No!"

Caroline froze. She had heard those words, that anguish, not from the Kaleidoscope Room, but in her bed—the words of Jared's nightmare.

"No!" she shouted, breaking the spell that had paralyzed her. "Jared, don't open—"

She reached him just as he finally got the stubborn door open, and they both froze in shock. Translucent images, shades of people who'd once been real, spread out before them. A dark-haired woman, finely dressed, lay on the floor, her neck at a grotesque angle. A giant of a man lay next to her, deathly still, blood thick in his strawberry-blond hair, eyes staring in a blank gaze into a black void of eternity. And kneeling next to the woman, a man wept as though his very heart had been rent from his chest.

In an instant, the tableau was gone, leaving Caroline and Jared wondering if it had ever really been there at all. A gust of wind swooshed through the room and dissipated, leaving behind only the scents of lavender and shaving soap and something stale and musty, like decaying moss—the smell of utter despair.

Caroline was the first to move; she stepped next to Jared and slipped her arms around his waist. He exhaled a sigh and wrapped his arms around her shoulders, clinging to her as fiercely as she clung to him.

THEY REMAINED THERE, embracing, for an indeterminably long time. Finally, Caroline said, "Your plan worked. You heard them for yourself."

"I got more than I bargained for," Jared said gravely.

"Now what?"

"I'm fresh out of ideas."

"We could run screaming through the streets," Caroline suggested.

"I'm sure that would make me feel better," Jared said sarcastically.

"You're the genius with all the plans."

It was a while before Jared spoke again. "I think we need to talk about what we saw." He pushed her hair aside and kissed her temple. "Do you want to go somewhere else, somewhere besides this house?"

Her cheek rubbed the front of his shirt as she shook her head. "I can't explain it. I'm shaken, but I'm not scared. I don't care where we are, so long as you keep on holding me."

"I feel the same way."

They wound up in Jared's suite, cuddled together on the sofa. "You were right," Jared said. "Katherine didn't die in the derailment. She died in this house."

"Not by Samuel's hand," Caroline said.

"By her lover's."

He sounded so forlorn and disillusioned that Caroline wished she had a magic salve for that part of him that had believed in his grandfather's idealized image of Katherine: beautiful, gentle, perfect. But the only salve she had to offer was the love she had for him, and she applied it in the form of a hug.

"It's all so incredible," Jared said. "No one knew. No one ever suspected. My grandfather didn't, I'm sure of that."

"It must have happened just before she was supposed to leave for Tallahassee. Otherwise, she would have been missed."

"He must have done something with the bodies. He must have been going crazy wondering what to tell people when she didn't show up in Tallahassee."

"And then fate stepped in," Caroline said. "The train derailed, and the cars carrying twenty-one members of a young ladies' choir exploded, and he had the perfect cover. No questions, no scandal, no investigation. Just the perfect tragic death for a woman who'd been a legend in her own time and could remain a legend for all time."

"I guess there's no way of knowing who the man was, or why he suddenly killed her. The way she laughed with him, danced with him—"

He looked into Caroline's eyes, searching for understanding and empathy. Finding it, he continued. "Maybe I just don't want to believe she was promiscuous, but from what we heard, it wasn't their first time. He wasn't a stranger. But if he wasn't, then she must have known him, and if she knew him, other people must have known him. Surely he'd have been missed."

"He was."

Jared tensed. "What do you know?"

"His name was Sven Yorick. He was the ice man. He disappeared that week. There was speculation that he might have been on the train, but no one saw him board, and none of the bodies matched his."

"How did you find out about him?"

"There was an article in the paper. And then, I asked Aunt Essie if she remembered him, and it all fell into place—except, of course, why he killed her."

"What did Aunt Essie tell you?"

"That Sven was a hunk."

"You think Katherine would have sacrificed her marriage for a hunk who delivered ice?"

"When you think of Katherine as a human being and not as a saint, it makes sense, Jared. Samuel gave her everything she needed. He even educated her. But he was sixty years old, and she was twenty-seven. She'd never been with anyone young and virile. No matter how much she cared for Samuel, she must have wondered. And then there was Sven, broad-chested and beautiful, and at his peak."

"I can see why she'd look and . . . fantasize. But to be unfaithful—"

"It's the unforgivable sin to you, isn't it?"

"She was his *wife!* He did so much for her."

"And she must have been aware every waking moment how much she owed Samuel Taggart. It couldn't have been easy living with that kind of indebtedness."

"So she had an affair with the ice man?"

"She was vulnerable, Jared. And Sven was there."

After an extended silence, Caroline said, "Sven was a giant of a man. Six-foot-six. I wonder how Samuel managed to overpower him."

"Maybe he surprised him," Jared speculated.

"He was enraged, too. People have been known to have extraordinary strength at times of extreme agitation."

Beneath her ear, Jared's chest vibrated with laughter, and the next thing Caroline knew, Jared was shifting, and guiding her into position so that he could kiss her. It was a sweet kiss that bespoke affection.

"What was that for?" she asked, smiling.

"For you. For the way you are. For the way you approach things from all angles, trying to be so objective and analytical-intellectual in your interpretation."

"I'm not sure," she said. "Is that good or bad?"

"If I were accused of a crime, I'd want you on the jury hearing the case."

There was another silence.

"How do you suppose he got the bodies downstairs?" Caroline asked at last.

Jared hadn't been thinking about Samuel. He'd been thinking about Caroline, and how good it was to have her there with him. He was a bit disappointed that *she* was thinking about Samuel again. "Hmm?"

"The bodies. Katherine was petite. It would have been rough, but he could probably have handled a woman her size. But Sven—the man was a giant. Six-foot-six, and broad. There are no indications that Samuel was athletic or even particularly physical. Do you think he had an accomplice, a faithful servant, maybe?"

Jared sat straight up, nearly knocking Caroline off the couch. "My God."

Caroline managed to resettle herself without falling off the couch. "Jared?"

"He couldn't have gotten those bodies downstairs!"

"Then—?"

Jared's gaze met hers, his eyes revealing an almost-painful intensity. He spoke with a chilling evenness of speech. "Maybe he wasn't much of a carpenter, either."

Caroline literally felt the blood leaving her face. "Oh, Jared, you don't think . . . you can't believe—"

"He moved downstairs, Caroline. He never went up there again. He couldn't *bear* to be up there. Everyone said so." After a painful pause, he sighed wearily. "We have to find out."

"Jared, we can't. If it's true, maybe it would be better—"

"To let sleeping dogs lie?" Jared asked.

"I wasn't going to say that," Caroline answered. "I was going to say that, if those bodies have been there over sixty years, maybe we shouldn't disturb them."

"And maybe we should."

"I don't know, Jared. And frankly, I'm glad it's your house and she's your relative. That makes it your call."

Jared took her hands in his. "Do you remember telling me that Katherine might have revealed herself because she was tired of the guilt?"

Caroline nodded.

"Maybe it wasn't that so much as that she was tired of being punished."

"Punished?"

"How would you like being walled up in a window seat with your lover, while another woman was buried in your grave next to your husband?"

"How can someone who's dead like or dislike anything?"

"How can someone who's dead dance and make love?"

Caroline buried her face in her hands and groaned wearily. "I don't want to think about any of this."

"I agree," Jared said.

Caroline looked up at his face, surprised. "You do."

He rose from the sofa. "Absolutely. We're not going to change almost seventy years of history in a few hours. Kath-

erine and Samuel and this . . . Sven character are dead and
gone, but we're alive. . . ."

He held out his hand in invitation. Caroline placed hers in
it and stood, facing him. Jared slipped his hands up her arms
and rested them on her shoulders. "We're here together, and
we're in love. The only thing I want to think about for the rest
of the night is you. And I don't want to share you—body or
mind—with any ghosts."

Caroline slid her fingers into his hair and smiled. "I'm sure
a resourceful man like you can think of a way to hold my interest."

"I'm going to give it my damnedest, Sugar Lips!" he promised, lowering his face to hers.

13

CAROLINE AWOKE TO FIND Jared propped up against the pillows, talking on the telephone. "I don't want to go into it now, Chief. You'll understand when you get here. I know, and I appreciate— Okay, I'll see you then. Thanks, Chief."

He replaced the receiver, and bent over to kiss Caroline on the nose. "Good morning, sleepyhead."

Caroline pushed up on one elbow. "What time is it?"

"Eight-thirty."

Yawning, Caroline murmured, "I can't believe I slept so late." After the experience in the Kaleidoscope Room, she hadn't expected to sleep at all. But Jared's lovemaking had provided sweet and total distraction. Afterward, she had felt so replete and safe in his arms, she hadn't given the Kaleidoscope Room or its ghosts another thought. "Who's up and accepting calls this early?"

"The chief of police," Jared said.

Caroline wondered if she should shake her head to clear away the cobwebs. "Of Taggartville?"

"Yes," Jared replied, grinning at her obtuseness. "I want an official present when we open that window seat."

"You've definitely decided to open it, then?"

"Yes. In about two hours." He looked at the sheet stretched across her breasts. "You might want to put on some clothes for the big event. I'm inviting that reporter, Jeff, and Aunt Essie, too."

"Why?" Caroline asked.

"If Katherine Taggart's up there, we can't just leave her in the window seat."

"I mean, why can't you just do it quietly? Why do you have to make it into a legal, media and historical event?"

"I'm not making it into anything. You don't just dig up sixty-year-old bodies and bury them in the backyard. There are legal ramifications to deal with, whether we want to or not."

He wrapped his hand around hers. "Trust my instincts on this, Caroline. I grew up in my grandfather's limelight. If we try to hide this or veil it in secrecy, there's going to be a lot of speculation and rumor mongering. In the end we'll be a lot better off if we're up-front about it."

"You, you mean."

He gave her a puzzled look, and she clarified, "You keep saying 'we,' but it's your house and your relative and your decision to be up-front. Not ours."

"You're involved in this up to those pretty eyeballs of yours, whether you like it or not."

"I'm your witness, you mean. The highly credible, objective observer."

"What's eating you, Caroline?"

"I don't know what you mean." But she did. She was in a situation from which there was no escape, and she was frustrated.

"There's enough hostility floating from your side of the bed to mine to start a war in a Third World country," Jared said. "I didn't dream up this ghost business, and the prospect of finding my great-aunt's body in a window seat in my cupola doesn't hold a lot of appeal for me."

Clutching the sheet to her, Caroline climbed out of bed and looked around for her clothes. "It's not going to hurt your tearoom or bed-and-breakfast business, though, is it? What's a Victorian mansion without a proper ghost?"

Finding the shirt she'd been wearing the night before, she yanked it on. "You know what irritates me, Jared? It's the way you always land on your feet."

"What the hell is that supposed to mean?" He climbed out of bed, too, without bothering with the sheet.

Caroline begrudged him the cocksureness of being able to stand there buck naked and magnificent and not feel self-conscious. "You're like a cat!" she fumed. "Most people with ghosts have to move out of the house they've invested all their money in and declare bankruptcy. Most people who have a family scandal based on adultery and murder and a cover-up would suffer from it, especially when they're trying to launch a political career. But this is just going to put patina on that silver spoon that's been sticking out of your mouth since birth, isn't it? It's going to enhance your charisma and make great copy. Hell, Jared, why stop at governor? Maybe your Great-Aunt Katherine will carry you all the way to the White House!"

Jared sniffed with an air of indignant superiority. "A bit testy this morning, aren't we?"

Caroline, who'd jerked on her pants, was fighting with a zipper, which was caught. She paused long enough to give him a withering glare. "You'd be testy, too, if you were in my position."

"Zippers can be a real bitch, all right."

"That's it. Crack cute little jokes. You're going to be here giving guided tours of the haunted cupola on your way to the governor's mansion, and I'm going to Boston, where I'll be that decorator who heard the ghosts down in that Florida mansion. It's not exactly the way I've always dreamed of becoming famous." After a beat, she corrected, "*Infamous.*"

Jared looked as though he wanted to say something, but had been rendered speechless.

Caroline cranked her chin a half inch higher. "If I've got to face the law, the press and Aunt Essie, I'm going to take a bath first."

Giving up on the zipper, she gathered the fronts of her shorts together in her fist and stomped out of the room.

Jared followed as far as the doorway and yelled at her re-
treating back, "Obviously I should have made coffee!"

THE THING CAROLINE MISSED most about a shower was the
ease of shampooing her hair. She'd had to develop a routine
of getting into an empty tub, wetting and sudsing her hair,
rinsing it under the tap, putting in conditioner, filling the tub
and soaking, emptying the tub and rinsing the conditioner
out.

She was in the soaking stage when she heard the knock on
her bedroom door.

"Caroline?" It was Jared's voice.

"I'm in the tub, Jared. I'll be out in ten minutes."

She heard the door hinges creak.

"I'm in the tub, Jared," she repeated. "Go away."

Footsteps. Getting closer. Mortified, Caroline slunk down
in the water to her neck. Fantasy was sitting in a bathtub filled
with bubbles with your hair tied atop your head with curls
cascading over a colorful ribbon. Reality was sitting in soap-
clouded water with your hair filled with gooey conditioner.

Jared, of course, was impeccably dressed, in white pants,
suspenders, and a wine-and-white-striped shirt with white
collar and cuffs. Every hair was in place. Jared, Caroline
knew, didn't even have to blow-dry his hair. He just towel-
blotted, combed, and it air-dried in total conformity with
current fashion.

There were times when she didn't like Jared a whole lot.
This was one of them. She crossed her arms over her breasts
and hoped the water was deep and murky enough to guard
her privacy elsewhere. From the glint in Jared's eyes, she suspected the water wasn't quite deep or soapy enough.

She scowled at him defiantly. "I think it's only fair to warn
you that I'm imagining what a volley of soapy water would
do to the disgustingly sharp crease in those nauseatingly
white pants."

He'd been holding one arm behind his back, and he whipped it around, producing a steaming mug of coffee. He extended his arm, holding the mug within her reach. "Emergency situations call for drastic measures."

"Just put it on the floor and get out!"

"We *are* in a state this morning, aren't we?"

"*We* are always in a state when men show up in our bathroom unannounced."

"Does this happen to you often?"

She answered with a scowl.

"Would you like me to scrub your back before I go?"

"And get those white cuffs all soggy?"

"I could roll them up."

"Don't bother."

Jared heaved an exaggerated, aggrieved sigh. "Chivalry gets a man nowhere in this day and age."

"Jared—"

"I'm going. But there's something I want to tell you before I go."

Caroline steeled herself. One crack about her hair, or any portion of her anatomy, and he was going to experience a tidal wave of epic bathtub proportions.

He just stood there, staring at her, until she thought she'd burst from sheet aggravation. "Well?" she prompted.

"You're one of the most exasperating women on the face of the earth. In fact, sometimes you're a grouch. But I love you, and I don't want you to go back to Boston and be the infamous ghost lady. I want you to stay here and marry me. Think about it."

With that, he stalked toward the door.

"Jared?" she croaked, her voice barely a whisper.

"Don't even consider answering me until you've finished that coffee," he said, without even breaking stride.

Caroline's jaw dropped. That was just like Jared Colin. Just like him! To come into the bathroom and propose marriage to her when she was stark-naked and her hair was full of conditioner! She ought to marry him just to get even. *Payback is hell, Jared Colin.*

Marry him! My God, what was she thinking? The man not only lived in a fishbowl, he thrived on it!

But he loves you.

He was launching a political career, which meant his wife would have to live in a fishbowl, too.

Do you have anything to hide?

He was spoiled rotten.

So he's rich . . . He's also generous and thoughtful.

He uses everything to his own advantage, from the house he inherited down to the ghosts haunting it.

So he's resourceful . . . Are you going to fault him for that?

He's too good-looking! The man's hair just combs into place!

You'd have beautiful children.

Caroline yanked the stopper from the drain with her big toe. If anything could bring her down from the clouds of fantasy to the bumpy road of reality, it was the image of an incorrigible three-year-old miniature Jared Colin. He'd be willful and single-minded and—Caroline sighed. He'd be absolutely adorable, and he'd charm the pants off his mother and father and any other adult he came into contact with.

The last of the bathwater gurgled down the drain, and she turned on the spigot and adjusted the water so she could rinse her hair. Soaking her head somehow seemed particularly apropos at that moment.

By the time she'd finished with her hair and dressed, she heard footfalls on the stairs again. She stepped from her suite into the hallway just in time to see Jared and another man reach the landing. The stranger was carrying two metal suitcaselike valises.

"Caroline!" Jared exclaimed, as though surprised to see her. As though he hadn't been in her bathroom less than an hour before while she was sitting in the tub in her altogether and proposed marriage to her. "I want you to meet Chris Cunningham. Chris is a free-lance video photographer. I asked him here to film the big event."

He turned to the photographer. "Caroline is one of the key players in our little drama."

Chris put down one of the cases to shake hands with Caroline. "Maybe you'll give me a hint what all this is about. Jared's being so secretive."

"It'll be easier to tell everyone at one time," Jared interjected. "Right now, you probably want to check out the lighting situation upstairs. The stained glass may create some special problems."

Chris shrugged his shoulders as if to say, "Oh, well," then picked up the metal cases and followed Jared to the Kaleidoscope Room.

Jared was so cool, so focused on the meeting ahead that Caroline wondered if she were going crazy and had imagined that he'd been in her bathroom proposing marriage. Then, from the top of the narrow stairway where he'd opened the door to the Kaleidoscope Room and was holding it while Chris maneuvered his cases through, Jared smiled down at her, and even from that distance, the expression in his eyes reiterated everything he'd said in the bathroom.

Self-conscious, suddenly, Caroline forced a half smile, then looked away, unable to deal with the intensity of his inquiring gaze as a flush rose in her cheeks. A fortuitous knock at the front door provided a convenient escape. "I'll get it," she volunteered.

Everyone else, it seemed, had arrived at the same time. Aunt Essie, Jeff Adams and the police chief were chatting companionably when Caroline answered the door. Caroline greeted them, introduced herself to the chief, and invited everyone to follow her upstairs.

In the Kaleidoscope Room, Caroline and Jared's apprehension over the task ahead butted against the strained curiosity of the observers—witnesses—Jared had summoned to the scene. Jared had put a disc on the Victrola—an upbeat orchestral rendition of "My Blue Heaven"—but still the tension was almost palpable as Aunt Essie, the chief of police and the young reporter settled into the chairs Jared had brought up from the dining room. The videographer peered through the lens of the camera he'd mounted on a tripod, and restlessly checked, then unnecessarily rechecked, knobs and dials and connections on his lighting equipment.

Caroline stood near Jared, ill at ease to find herself near center stage in a drama that had begun almost seven decades earlier. Jared waited for the end of the record before lifting the stylus. He paused dramatically, then said, "I suppose you're all wondering why I invited you here."

Titters of laughter did not totally defeat the tension in the room. "You may have heard some rumors about strange goings-on at Katherine House in recent weeks."

"Strange goings-on, or hanky-panky?" Jeff asked wryly.

Jared tensed, but didn't lose his composure. "It's strange you should mention hanky-panky," he said, "because we're going to be discussing that, too, but not in the way you think."

He'd captured their full attention again. "Just over two weeks ago, I attended a meeting at the Cow Café. While I was gone, Caroline heard what she believed to be two people in the Kaleidoscope Room. This is what she heard."

As he turned on the tape recorder, he told Caroline, "Signal when we reach the point where you turned on Sousa."

Caroline watched the expressions on the faces of the others turn from curiosity to rapt interest, wondering how Aunt Essie would react to the heavy breathing. She was relieved to see that the older woman took it with equanimity.

She nodded at the appropriate time, and Jared switched off the recorder. "At this point, Caroline assumed that I had returned home and was—uh—entertaining in the Kaleidoscope Room."

More titters. Jared paused until they'd subsided before continuing. "Being the soul of tact that she is, she then began playing marches by John Philip Sousa in order to alert me to the fact that my. . . lapse of discretion was being overheard. When I actually did return home, I heard the Sousa, but didn't know why she was playing it so loudly. When we finally compared notes and realized there had been a misunderstanding, we assumed there had been prowlers in the house, and I installed new security locks on the doors."

He stopped to catch his breath before picking up the story. "A week later, I went out again—"

He went on to relate how Caroline had heard the same sounds and, thinking the prowlers had returned, telephoned the police, who investigated and found no one or nothing amiss.

"She attributed the noises to mice, but she didn't think what she heard were mice. She was beginning to suspect that what she was hearing was supernatural."

"Are you trying to tell us this old house is haunted?" Jeff asked, as though he'd been torn from hot news for a scam. The videographer looked equally skeptical.

"You'll have to make your own judgment on that, Jeff," Jared said. "But I hope you'll hear us out."

He went on with the story, playing the rest of the tape when appropriate, describing the morbid tableau they'd seen in the Kaleidoscope Room, aptly leading the witnesses step by step through the events and logic that had led to the hypothesis that the remains of Katherine Taggart and Sven Yorick might be sealed in the window seat.

Everyone was skeptical, but intrigued. Jared invited them to examine the window seat and the nails sealing it. "We may have brought all of you out for nothing," he concluded, "but if we should find bodies here, we wanted the story of how we came to discover them documented."

"You called us here to watch you open it?" This from the chief of police.

Jared reached behind the Victrola for the crowbar he'd brought upstairs, and offered it to the chief. "I was hoping you'd do the honors, Chief."

Nodding, the chief took the tool.

Jared turned to Aunt Essie. "Aunt Essie, you've heard it all. You can stay, or you can go."

Aunt Essie snorted indignantly. "I'm no frail old lady, Jared Colin. I've buried my parents, my siblings, a son and my husband. You don't have to worry about me keeling over at the sight of a skeleton or two. I've sat through the preliminaries on this hard wooden chair. I'm not about to leave before the main event."

Jared raised an eyebrow at the videographer in inquiry. The photographer gave him a thumbs-up sign. Jeff had unpacked his still camera, as well. "I'm set, too, Jared."

Jared stepped behind Caroline and placed his hands on her shoulders reassuringly. "You ready?"

"Yes," she said, raising her hand to cover Jared's where it rested on her left shoulder.

The chief positioned the crowbar, and an odd hush settled over the room as he hesitated; it was shattered when Aunt Essie admonished, "You be careful with that, buddy. There's no use defacing the wood any more than absolutely necessary."

The chief blushed. "Yes, ma'am. I'll be as careful as possible." Then, with a series of prying pumps, he loosened the lid enough to lift it with one final thrust. The old wood groaned and squeaked as the old nails were rent asunder.

Everyone stared into the well in reverent silence. Musty air, lavender-tinged and cloying, wafted up from that long-sealed cavity.

There should be noise, Caroline thought. *Hysteria, confusion, gasps of disbelief. We should all be screaming.* But there was only silence, and the empty eye sockets of a mummified face staring up at them.

Then the chief said, "Ho-lee shit!" and Chris almost knocked the tripod over in his haste to get the camera repositioned so he could aim the lens directly into the cavity, and Jeff was clicking away with his camera.

Caroline turned into Jared's arms. "She's really there."

She felt Jared's sigh in the vibration of his chest and the exhalation of breath that skittered through her hair. "I don't think I really believed it, either."

"Her hair's still curly," Aunt Essie said, dispassionately studying the corpse. "The few times I saw her, that hair always impressed me. Who'd have thought it would still be curly after all this time?"

"Is that a man's shoe behind her head?" Jared asked.

"Sure is," the chief replied. "Whoever put them there laid them head to foot and foot to head."

"Is there going to be a lot of red tape on this?" Jared asked.

"A crime this old should just be a matter of some paperwork, especially if we're careful to follow procedure. I'd like to get the county's mobile crime unit and the coroner's wagon over here before we disturb anything."

"Can I get a copy of that tape?" Jeff asked. "My editor's not going to believe this."

"I dubbed a couple of copies this morning," Jared said.

"There's no wedding ring on her finger," Caroline observed. "Samuel must have taken it off."

"No one ever suspected," Aunt Essie said. "Everyone knew Sven was involved with a married woman, but no one would ever have believed it was Katherine Taggart. And there was never a whisper of doubt that she died in that derailment."

"Until Katherine herself told us," Jared said.

IT WAS LATE AFTERNOON by the time the crime unit finished processing the scene and lifted Katherine's body from the window-seat well, revealing the male body underneath. Chief Wilson, who'd hovered over the deputies almost to the point of annoyance, knelt next to the seat well and pointed a flashlight toward the cadaver's head. Any residual doubts about the identity of Katherine's lover were erased by the thatch of strawberry-blond hair, still dirtied by blood that had turned to powder, protruding from the shriveled scalp stretched over the skull.

"Sven Yorick," Caroline said.

"Looks like it, from the description Aunt Essie gave us," Chief Wilson said.

While they'd waited on the crime team, there had been questions, endless questions, and theories and speculation, and Caroline had shown everyone the photocopy of the article about Sven. Aunt Essie, relishing the spotlight, had been forced to relate everything she remembered about Sven Yorick, and the ice man had emerged, in the telling, as a strawberry-blond cross between Rudolph Valentino and Arnold Schwarzenegger.

"Looks like a tall one, too," the chief noted as the deputies lifted the cadaver. "They'll measure him at the morgue. Whoa, what's this?" He turned to the deputy who'd been doing the official photographs. "Get a shot of this."

Jeff and the videographer moved in close, too, not wanting to miss anything significant.

"Jeez, you think that's the murder weapon?" the deputy asked.

"Looks like it," said the chief. "The proverbial fireplace poker."

"And very convenient," Caroline said. "The kind of thing a person would grab if he came into the house and heard his wife screaming for help."

The deputy picked up the poker and examined the pointed tip. "He must have wiped it clean. The lab'll find any traces of blood. Don't know why we're even bothering with something this old, though. It's not as though we're going to clear it with an arrest."

"There's going to be an avalanche of publicity on this. The inquiring minds of our taxpaying citizens are going to want to know every detail we can give them. It's your chance to shine, Deputy," the chief said.

"Hey, is that a book?"

"It's one of Katherine's journals," Caroline said, reaching for it without thinking, only to find Jared's hand on her arm, stopping her, and the chief and the deputy looking at her as though she'd just tried to pull the dagger from a murder victim's back.

"That's evidence," the deputy growled.

"I'm sorry," Caroline said, embarrassed. "It's just . . . I've been reading Katherine's journals."

Jared turned to the chief. "I've got a copy machine downstairs. Would it be okay if we copied the text before you took the book?"

"It wouldn't be procedure," the deputy replied.

Jared frowned. "You said yourself this isn't an ordinary case. It's not going to make the difference between making an arrest or not making one. Even if you dusted it and found prints after all these years, you wouldn't have Taggart's or Yorick's prints to match them with."

"There has to be some reason it was sealed up in here with them," the deputy reasoned.

"That's why I'm interested in reading it," Caroline said. "I've read all the others." When the deputy showed no signs of relenting, she added, frustrated, "Damn it, I'm the one who kept hearing the ghosts. If not for that, we'd never even have found the bodies."

"You'll have the book itself," Jared said. "It's the text we're interested in." He looked at the chief. "Eventually it'll make its way back to me, anyway."

The deputy set his jaw petulantly, and the chief snorted derisively. "Oh, lighten up, deputy. He's right. Technically it belongs to him, even if it is evidence. Miss Naylor might even be willing to read the text and prepare a summary. Since she's been reading the other volumes, she might spot irregularities we'd miss."

Reluctantly the deputy nodded. "But I'm going to supervise the photocopying."

Jared went with them as well, since he knew how to operate the machine and fill the paper trough. Caroline thumbed through the journal while they waited for the machine to warm up. "It's Katherine's handwriting."

They quickly developed a routine of page turning, positioning on the screen and copying, and less than half an hour later, they reached the last entry. "This is strange," Caroline said, staring down at the page.

Jared and the deputy both looked at her. She held out the journal so they could read the final entry. "It's not Katherine's handwriting."

The heavy script, uneven as though it had been written by a trembling hand, said: "Katherine Taggart murdered by Sven Yorick. May she rest in peace. Sven Yorick executed by Samuel Taggart. May he burn in hell."

It was dated the day before the derailment, the eve of Katherine's scheduled departure for Tallahassee.

"This pretty much confirms all the theories," the deputy said. "It's just a formality, but do you have a sample of Old Man Taggart's handwriting?"

"I'm sure we can find one," Jared said.

Having finished copying the journal, Caroline surrendered it to the deputy and excused herself, saying she'd like a few minutes alone in her suite. Catching Jared's eye, she indicated the stack of photocopies she had collected from the machine. "Do you want these?"

"Take them," he said. "I know you're dying to read them."

For a while, she just lay on her bed. She was weary, but not physically tired, and it felt good doing nothing for those few minutes except let her mind wander at will over the extraordinary events that had been part of her life at Katherine House.

Ghosts. Haunted dreams. Bodies in the window seat. Crimes of passion. What had happened to her well-ordered life and the job that had grown so mundane that she was considering looking around for something more challenging? This job was supposed to have been simple and fun—an interlude for relaxation and reevaluation.

Desdemona, ever alert to the prospect of a little attention, jumped up on the bed. Caroline scratched the cat's neck, "Well, Dessie, it certainly hasn't been dull, has it?"

Dessie tilted her head back and purred. Predictably, after a few moments of having her chest stroked, she dozed off. Caroline sighed, envying the cat her feline obliviousness. She herself couldn't have fallen asleep if her life depended on it.

Spying the photocopied journal pages, she picked them up and began reading.

14

AT LAST, EVERYONE LEFT, taking with them their cameras and evidence kits and crime vans and body wagons. Jared closed the door behind the police chief, and sucked a fortifying draft of air into his lungs. Although he longed to talk to Caroline, as much to sop reassurance from her voice as to assure himself that she was all right, he had one chore to attend to before he allowed himself that privilege.

Sinking into the chair behind his desk, he picked up the phone and pressed one of the memory buttons. Then, after a few rings, he said, "Mother. Yes, it's Jared. Listen, something's come up and I thought you'd want to be prepared—"

Probably because he'd been immersed in the situation all day, the telling of it was even more arduous than he'd anticipated. His mother reacted with predictable incredulity, doubt and questions. He answered the latter with as much patience as he could muster after the trying day. He owed his family that much, considering what the press would be putting them through in the next few days.

"Is there anything else?" he heard his mother ask.

For the first time in several hours, Jared grinned. "There is one other thing, but it's personal. It's not for publication."

A pause followed.

"The girl I mentioned, Caroline Naylor."

"The decorator," his mother said.

"I asked her to marry me this morning."

"You what? Jared, how can you add that as a . . . a . . . footnote?"

"Don't worry. You'll love her as much as I do. She's smart and beautiful, and comes from good stock. Her father's native Floridian and an acclaimed scientist, and her mother's Boston Brahmin."

"When are we going to meet her?" his mother pressed. "And when's the wedding?"

"Calm down, Mother. She hasn't said yes, yet."

"I thought you said she was smart."

"She is," Jared said. "But she's a little on the cantankerous side."

"It's beginning to sound like a match made in heaven," Mrs. Colin said drolly.

After hanging up the phone, Jared sat at his desk for a few minutes, listening to the silence. Following the confusion of the day, Katherine House, at early dusk, was empty and eerily still, like a long-abandoned cave, or a long-forgotten tomb. And the owner of Katherine House suddenly felt very much alone.

He stood at the door to Caroline's suite, hesitating, debating whether he should knock, wondering if he would be invading her privacy if he did. She must have known everyone else was gone, yet she hadn't come downstairs. Nor had she left the door of her suite ajar, as if to invite him in. Maybe the closed door was her way of saying she'd like some privacy.

But, needing her, he knocked, and then suffered a purgatory of waiting before the door was opened and her eyes met his. They were red-rimmed and puffy, and her cheeks were stained with tears. Before he could ask her why, her arms were around his neck, her face buried in the crook of his shoulder, her body nestled against his with a beseeching wriggle that begged for comfort.

"She was pregnant. After years of wanting Samuel's child, she was pregnant with Sven's."

"Is that why he killed her?"

"No. He didn't know about the baby. He was very jealous of Samuel. He wanted Katherine to go away with him, but she was going to try to talk him into leaving alone. She wanted to stay with Samuel and let him believe the child was his. She loved him, and wanted to give him the child he'd always wanted."

"Even if it wasn't his."

"She knew a child would make him happy. It was something no one else could give him. And Jared, she was afraid of Sven. He was very possessive and had a terrible temper. He scared her. That's another reason she was hoping to talk him into leaving. She knew as long as he was in Taggartville, he'd never leave her alone. She was even going to offer him her jewelry, and if he still wouldn't agree, she was going to offer to take money from Samuel's safe."

"But Sven wouldn't agree, and killed her when she refused to leave with him, and Samuel came in just in time to see it happen. Did he know about her and Sven?"

"If he did, Katherine didn't know about it. It was her greatest fear that he would find out. It was just as we surmised, that she became infatuated with Sven. He would come over on Thursday nights when Samuel was at his lodge meeting. But after a while, he wanted more from her."

She sighed. "We'll never know whether the meeting broke up early that night because of the weather, or whether he came home purposely in order to check on Katherine. Either way—"

"Either way, what happened, happened."

Still locked in an embrace, they fell into a thoughtful silence. Then, abruptly, Jared said, "This house is as depressing as a tomb. Let's get out of here for a while."

They drove aimlessly down the interstate, and finally stopped at a café on a little lake just outside Orlando, and watched the sun set over the water from their patio table as they ate. As the last of the reflected rays sank into the darkness of the water, Jared squeezed her hand and said, "Thank God this day is finally over."

Caroline was touched. Through it all he'd been stoic, composed and in control. She'd wondered if he'd really felt so little at seeing the body of his great-aunt. Now, he was allowing her to see that he had been more affected than he would let anyone else know.

Reading Katherine's private journal had been an emotionally wrenching experience, especially following the exhumation in the Kaleidoscope Room, and Katherine was still on Caroline's mind.

"I wonder..." she murmured. And when Jared expressed an interest in what she was wondering, she told him: "Katherine was pregnant, and it was warm, and her fingers were so swollen that she had to take off her wedding band. She had a special velvet box for it. If she'd been wearing it when Samuel put her in the window seat, I wonder if he'd have been able to pull off that false identification. I wonder if he'd even have tried it."

"He must have gone through hell," Jared said. "Keeping that secret, living with the truth and his own falsehood."

"You always related to Samuel," she said. "Even though you and I had danced the way Katherine and Sven danced, it was Samuel you related to. Your nightmares were his nightmares."

His eyes, filled with love, met hers. "Samuel was the one who loved her."

Unable to deal with the intensity of that loving gaze, Caroline closed her eyes and took a steeling breath.

"I'm sick of Katherine and Samuel and Sven and that stupid train wreck," Jared said.

"Then let's not talk about it anymore," Caroline said, opening her eyes. "Let's talk about the weather or traffic or the President's trip to Europe."

"I've got a better idea," Jared said, taking enough cash from his pocket to cover the meal and putting it on the check on the table. He stood and reached down for her hand. "Let's take a walk around the lake in the moonlight and talk about us."

Hand in hand they walked, listening to the lapping of the water in the breeze and the concert of bullfrogs and the occasional splash of a fish jumping. Ducks huddled at the water's edge, their feathers ruffled out against the cool night air. The mildly undulating surface of the lake caught the light of the half-moon and reflected it back in a fluted, fun-house mirror image.

On the far shore, as distant from the lights of the café and the street as they could get, they stopped. Jared picked up a pebble and skipped it across the water, then watched the reflected moonlight dance in the ripples created when it sank.

"I asked you to marry me this morning. Have you thought about it?"

"Of course, I have."

"And?"

"And I'm... Jared, you can't ask me to make a decision like that in a few hours, especially under such extraordinary circumstances."

"Love has nothing to do with circumstances, Caroline. You feel love, you don't analyze it."

"Jared, you're asking me to change my entire life."

"I'm asking you to share it with someone who loves you— who wants to share his life with you."

"You can't make that kind of judgment in just a few weeks."

"Maybe *you* can't," he said sadly. "I think I made that judgment the moment I saw you get out of your car. I didn't know who you were. I didn't know you were the decorator I'd hired. All I knew was that you were special. And when you looked at me, don't tell me you didn't feel something, too— something special."

"Chemistry," she said. "Attraction. A woman's appreciation of a good-looking man."

"Is that all? Can you honestly say that, Caroline? What about the times we waltzed together? What about when we made love? That couldn't possibly all be simple chemistry."

"No. But I can't be sure that it's love, either—the right kind of love, anyway."

"Love doesn't come with time limitations," Jared said. "Samuel knew he loved Katherine in a single glance."

"That's not the most persuasive argument you could use after the day we've had. Look where they ended up."

"Look at the happiness they shared despite it."

Caroline met Jared's gaze directly. "The entire time we've known each other we've been caught up in the romance of Katherine House. How can I know—how can either of us know—whether what you felt was for me, or whether you would have felt that way about any girl you were dancing with."

"Is that what you think? That everything we've shared has been just reaction to time and place and mood?"

"Not everything," she said. "We've already established that's there was some strong chemistry between us from the very beginning."

Jared grasped her upper arms. "What I feel for you is more than chemistry, and it's not just some romantic whimsy that comes from dancing with you at three o'clock in the morning. It's love, Caroline. Plain and simple. It's not just chemistry or romantic settings, it's you. It's Caroline Naylor. I've never felt this way about a woman before."

"You've never been advised to find the 'right' woman and get married before, either."

"Is that what this is all about?"

"Maybe not consciously," Caroline said. "But subconsciously... Face it, Jared, I could have been sent over from central casting. You were only half joking that night we discussed my résumé."

"I've had plenty of women interested in becoming Mrs. Jared Colin, Caroline. If I were looking for an arm ornament to enhance my political career, I could call up any one of several women I know who'd be more than delighted—and qualified—to fill that position."

He waited for her to reply. She didn't. "The point is," he continued, "I don't want just a suitable woman. I want the woman I'm in love with."

His hands were still loosely cupped around her arms, and he raised his right hand to caress her cheek with his fingers. "I don't want an arrangement or a deal. I could have had that six months ago when the committee made their recommendations. I want a wife and a marriage and a family."

Her eyes were bright. "Oh, Jared."

"That's the way I like to hear you say my name," he said.

"Don't do this to me, please. I do . . . I am in love with you. I'm just not sure that I can be the woman you need. And if I'm not, we'd both be unhappy."

"How could you possibly not be the woman I need, when I want you so badly?"

"Because you live in a fishbowl, and I'm not sure I can do that. What if I try and I can't? What if I hate it—all the press, and the parties, and the smiling at people you don't respect, and the wheeling and dealing. What if you change, and I don't like the man you become? What if I change, and neither of us likes the woman I become? What if I'm so miserable there's no chance either of us could be happy?"

"We could give it a try," he said. "If being a political wife makes you unhappy, then I'll just have to get out of politics."

"But it's your life. It's what you want to do with your life."

"No, Caroline. It's one thing I could do, but it's not my only choice."

"And you'd give it up, for me?"

"In a heartbeat, Sugar Lips."

Caroline exhaled a shuddering sigh. "Hold me, Jared." *Give me your strength.*

"For the rest of our lives, if you'll let me," he said.

"I can't make that commitment yet—especially when we're standing in the moonlight and you've been saying such sweet things. I can't think straight in the moonlight."

"You do entirely too much thinking, anyway," Jared said, and kissed her.

They were quiet on the drive back to Taggartville. In fact, the first words uttered in the car after they'd left the lake were the swearwords Jared said when they approached Katherine House and spied a TV truck and several strange cars parked at the curb.

"What do they want?" Caroline asked.

"The story," Jared said flatly.

"At eight o'clock in the evening?"

"I believe this comes under the heading Fishbowl Existence." His eyes met hers. "You don't have to talk to them. You can go straight inside the house if you want to. I'll handle them."

Caroline put her hand over his and squeezed it. "Like it or not, I think we're in this one together."

She moved to get out of the car, but Jared grabbed her hand. "Don't answer any personal questions, don't respond to anyone who's rude to you, and don't tell them anything that makes you uncomfortable." Caroline nodded. "Ready?" When she nodded again, he grinned and said, "Then let's go for a swim in that bowl."

Jared was in his element—Caroline saw that at once. He charmed the reporters with his frankness, his patience and his affable grin. He was open about the discovery of the bodies, sincere when he told the reporters he wasn't sure where the bodies would be buried, or what would become of the unknown derailment victim in Katherine Taggart's grave. He graciously refused to let them inside, to give them photo-copies of Katherine Taggart's journal or to answer any question regarding his personal relationship with Caroline, then invited them to come back at ten o'clock the next morning for an informal press conference, at which he would have prepared statements, photographs, and excerpts from the journal available.

And by the time he whisked Caroline through the front door of Katherine House, the press belonged to Jared Colin, the charismatic grandson of the late Mitchell Colin, former governor of Florida.

Inside the house, Jared and Caroline stood facing each other in the huge Grand Salon.

"You were great!" Jared said, smiling approval.

Caroline returned his smile. "I did okay, for an interior decorator. *You* were great."

An uncomfortable silence followed. Finally, Jared wrapped his arms around her. "I need your company tonight."

"I wouldn't want to be alone," she said, relaxing against him.

"I'm glad."

There were several messages on his machine. The first was from Chris, telling Jared he'd sold a free-lance piece on the ghosts to an Orlando station and that they should watch for it on the evening news. The others were all from reporters who'd read the story Jeff had filed on the news wire and wanted to schedule interviews.

"Are you going to call them back?" Caroline asked.

"Yes. At nine o'clock in the morning. I've got better things to do tonight."

"Like what?"

"Besides watching the eleven o'clock news?"

"Uh-hmm."

"I'm going to be very busy trying to convince the woman I love that she wants to spend the rest of her life with me."

He left the answering machine on immediate ring so they could screen calls instead of answering the phone. He opened a bottle of wine and toasted Katherine Taggart, and they sipped it while watching one of Jared's favorite movies on the VCR. At eleven, they switched off the movie and put in a new blank tape so they could record the news report.

After it aired, Jared watched it several times, pausing the recorder on a close-up of Caroline's face.

"Jared," Caroline said.

"Can you look at that face and wonder why I love you?"

She pummeled his arm playfully with her fist. "You're embarrassing me."

"I love it when you're rough!" he said, grinning lecherously. She raised her hand to pummel him again, and this time he caught her wrist on the downstroke to ward off the blow, and the next thing Caroline knew, she was flat on her back under him on the couch. A very long time later, they adjourned to his bed, where she slept soundly until morning.

When she awoke, the printer from Jared's computer was clicking away, and Caroline could hear the sloosh-groan-wheeze peculiar to his copier. She snitched a T-shirt from Jared's drawer and put it on, then sauntered into his office. "You're up early," she commented.

"Getting ready for our press conference," he said.

"Can I help?"

"I was hoping you'd ask. Can you pick a few excerpts from Katherine's journal to go into the press packets?"

"I've already flagged several passages."

"Damn, you're good!" He gave her that lady-killer smile. It was seven-thirty in the morning and he was cheerful and he looked as though he'd been spit shined from head to toe. And he loved her. "We make a hell of a team, Caroline."

"You're much too sparkly for me," she said dryly. *Could she spend the rest of her life with a man who looked that good at seven-thirty in the morning?* She was beginning to think she might!

Jared laughed. "I'll have coffee waiting when you get back downstairs."

THE PUBLIC PROVED TO HAVE an insatiable curiosity about ghosts and a soft spot for a true-life romantic tragedy. Jared continued distributing press kits but screened interview requests carefully.

There were a few prank calls, but there were also some nice letters and—to Caroline's consternation—fan mail. She received a call from a modeling agency wanting to know if she was interested in a modeling career, and flowers from a man she'd dated casually in high school and hadn't seen since. It took her a while to figure out that Dr. Gerald Nesbit was good old Gerry. Danitra and the gang from Urbane! sent a terse note that oozed envy over Caroline's sudden fame. And Jared's college buddy, Teddy Cross, made an appointment to talk about buying movie rights to the Katherine Taggart story.

Behind the scenes, Jared purchased a burial plot and stone in a local cemetery for Sven Yorick, and arranged for the body buried in Katherine Taggart's grave to be moved to the memorial cemetery at the Tragic Derailment site so Katherine could be interred next to Samuel as soon as the coroner released her body.

On the day of the transfer, he made a mysterious trip to the police station and returned with Katherine Taggart's wedding ring. "I asked them to get it so we can put it on Katherine's finger."

Caroline examined the ring, admiring the detail in the floral motif carved in the circle of gold. "Are these orange blossoms?"

"Yes. It was a custom design." He paused. "The coroner said there was no way it had been in a fire, and anyone who'd

seen it on a burn victim would have known it immediately—
even in 1930. Old Samuel's influence must have carried a lot
of clout."

Throughout the hubbub, Jared and Caroline attempted to
carry on their daily routines. The paper she'd specially ordered for the Garden Room arrived, and Caroline super-
vised the paperhangers who regarded her with the mixed awe
and curiosity with which they might regard a rock star or the
retired madam of a society bordello. Jared kept up his business interests in between interview requests.

They lunched at the Cow Café, and went wherever they
felt like for dinner. In one Orlando restaurant they were asked
for their autographs.

At night, they abided by an unspoken agreement not to
mention Katherine, Samuel, ghosts, murder, or cemeteries.
They played checkers, watched movies and read. They continued sleeping together, sometimes after heated, frenzied
lovemaking, sometimes after slow, tender lovemaking,
sometimes after a playful, erotic romp.

Jared told Caroline he loved her. He told her she was
beautiful. He told her she had the sexiest body in the world
and he loved every square inch of it. But he didn't mention
marriage again; he always stopped just short of mentioning
the future, or commitment, or marriage.

Plain and simple, he was waiting her out. Caroline knew
it and she loved him for it—for not pressuring her. And every
day, she got a bit closer to being ready to make that commitment.

Finally the call came that the coroner was releasing the
bodies. Aunt Essie asked if the society members might attend the interment, out of respect for Katherine Taggart's role
in the history of Taggartville. Jared agreed, and invited them
to a reception at Katherine House afterward.

While Caroline was on one phone line arranging for a caterer, Jared took a call on the second line. She saw him spring

to attention as he listened to the caller, and then give out the time and date of the interment, and the name of the funeral director handling the burial. They hung up from their respective calls within seconds of each other.

"I knew it!" Jared said elatedly. "Caroline, that was the producer of *Eye on Us*."

"Are you serious?"

"I knew it!" Jared repeated. "I knew if we kept refusing all those late-night television tabloids we'd hit pay dirt!"

"Pay dirt?"

"It's prime-time network, Caroline. Nothing tacky or sensational. Straight news! They're sending an entire crew."

A bigger fishbowl, Caroline thought, but it no longer bothered her. They'd been swimming in a fishbowl more chaotic than any political campaign ever could be, but Jared had made it bearable because he knew how to shut away the world at the end of the day and create a private world just for them. And the longer she knew him, the more convinced she became that he'd always be able to do that, no matter how big a fishbowl they swam in.

A major magazine—one of those that focused on personalities and trends more than on hard news but which had a reputation for getting the facts straight—also sent a reporter and photographer to the interment. Despite the news crews, it was a solemn occasion, treated by those who attended with the proper respect and decorum. A minister blessed the grave and read Scripture, and there was a moment of silence. And there were flowers—a surprising number of flowers sent by people who admired and respected the Colin family.

Jared's parents attended, which made Caroline tense, until Jared introduced her and she discovered how nice they were. Thanks to the efficiency of the caterer and Jared's charm in the role of host, the reception went smoothly.

Caroline was beginning to believe she might actually survive the dreadful day until Aunt Essie and a committee o three asked to see the window seat in the Kaleidoscope Room. Caroline held her breath, wondering how Jared could possibly refuse the request graciously.

Obviously, he couldn't, for he graciously invited everyone upstairs, begging their pardon for the confusion of the second floor, which was in the process of full renovation. So the party moved upstairs, albeit quite slowly, to accommodate arthritic joints.

Jared offered Caroline his elbow and extended his arm toward the stairs. "Shall we?"

"I thought I might skip this tour," she said.

"Aw, come on," he said, and she relented, accompanying him up the two flights.

She detected something amiss as soon as she walked in. Aunt Essie was holding court near the window seat, pointing and telling, and there were some involuntary cringes and shivers, but there was something else, a mood of hushed expectancy, as though everyone were waiting for something.

A ghost to materialize? she wondered wearily, and then thought, *That would really cork the bottle if Katherine decided to make an appearance following her burial.*

Jared made his way to the Victrola and wound it. Out of the corner of her eye, Caroline noted that the magazine team had followed the party, bulky cameras and all.

Jared seemed to find it appropriate to make a speech. "All of you have heard the story of Katherine Taggart's ghost by now—"

Caroline's mouth twitched with the urge to smile at how stately he sounded—how much like a politician. That was Jared, right smack-dab in the middle of the fishbowl and fluttering his fins.

"You've all heard about the woman who's been at the center of the action around here, too. Caroline, you're part of this. Please join me."

Slightly self-conscious, Caroline walked over to him. Surely he didn't expect her to give a speech, too.

"There's been a lot of speculation about the relationship between Miss Naylor and myself, and I'd like to go on record as saying that she is the most talented and competent decorator with whom I've ever had the pleasure of working."

Caroline fought to keep a straight face. She knew for a fact that Jared had never worked with a decorator before!

"Aunt Essie recommended Caroline for this job, and I hired her on the basis of that recommendation. So, Aunt Essie, thanks for the lead."

He's up to something, Caroline thought, as Aunt Essie enjoyed the spotlight Jared had cast her way.

"When we first came into this room," Jared continued, "Caroline told me that as a child, she'd fantasized about the colored lights dancing on the floor here. And it wasn't too many days later that Caroline and I danced together in this room to one of my Great-Aunt Katherine's old records."

Definitely up to something, Caroline realized, hoping that no one could see the flush she felt creeping up her neck and over her cheeks, as several members of the Taggartville Historical Preservation Society sighed.

"And it was in this room, that Caroline and I first kissed."

"Jared!" It escaped before she even knew she was going to say it.

Jared gave her that exasperating lady-killer smile. "You know I hate it when you say my name that way, Sugar Lips."

There were titters from the crowd, but they were eating it up. Oh, how he held that crowd! She might have admired it if she hadn't been so preoccupied contemplating giving the Taggartville Police Department and the county sheriff's department a new homicide to investigate.

"It's no surprise to anyone who's seen us together that I'm crazy in love with this woman."

She gave him an exasperated look, and found only a cocky grin on his face and a lot of love in his eyes. He spoke only to her. "I asked you once before to marry me, and you said you had to think it over. Now, I'm asking again in a roomful of witnesses. Will you marry me, Caroline Naylor?"

Caroline looked at Jared; she looked at the expectant faces of the members of the Taggartville Historical Preservation Society; and she looked into her own heart. And she knew that she couldn't disappoint anyone—not Jared, not the ladies of the society, and most of all, not herself.

"This is just like you," she mumbled just loud enough for Jared to hear.

"I think I missed that," Jared said.

"Yes," she whispered.

He cupped his hand to his ear, ear-horn-fashion, as though he hadn't heard. "Yes!" she said, loud enough for the entire room to hear.

There was a collective sigh. Scattered applause followed, and after that, the pop of a champagne cork and assorted giggles. "Thanks, Dad," Jared said, and Caroline followed his gaze to the back of the room, where Mr. Colin had just opened the bottle and was passing out champagne flutes.

"Before we pour the wine, I have one more bit of business to attend to, if I can find—" He was digging in his coat pocket. "Ah, yes." He held up a ring. "I took the liberty of having a mold cast from Katherine's ring, and commissioning a set."

Caroline's hand trembled as she held it out for him to slip the ring on her finger. Set in the center blossom was a round-cut diamond solitaire. Once the ring was in place, Jared kissed her finger, and then turned back to his father. "Okay, Dad. Pour the champagne while I dance with the future Mrs. Colin."

He put the stylus on the disc and led her around the room to the melody of "Three O'Clock in the Morning." They danced on and on, until they noticed a strange tittering in the

crowd, and Jared stopped. They followed the eyes of everyone in the room to the Victrola, where the stylus hit the
smooth area of the end of the disc and bounced back and
forth, and the Victrola suddenly emitted only a scratching
sound.

"It's been bouncing back and forth in that smooth area for
over a minute," someone said. "The record was over, but it
kept playing music."

The odd occurrence was destined to be discussed for years
to come, and everyone present formed an opinion or theory
about how the music kept on going after Jared Colin proposed to Caroline Naylor in the Kaleidoscope Room in front
of the ladies of the Taggartville Historical Preservation Society.

By far the most common explanation was that it was a toast
of good cheer to the happy couple from Katherine Taggart.
That, at least, was the theory put forth in the article in the
national magazine that sported Caroline's photo on its cover
the following week, along with the caption: Caroline Naylor—The Woman With The Most Romantic Love Story Of
The Century.

Rebels & Rogues

**Quade had played by their rules . . .
now he was making his own.**

**The Patriot
by Lynn Michaels
Temptation #405, August**

All men are not created equal. Some are rough
around the edges. Tough-minded but
tenderhearted. Incredibly sexy. The tempting
fulfillment of every woman's fantasy.

When it's time to fight for what they believe in, to
win that special woman, our Rebels and Rogues are
heroes at heart. Twelve Rebels and Rogues, one
each month in 1992, only from Harlequin
Temptation. Don't miss the upcoming books by
our fabulous authors, including Ruth Jean Dale,
Janice Kaiser and Kelly Street.

WELCOME TO

The quintessential small town where everyone knows everybody else!

Finally, books that capture the pleasure of tuning in to your favorite TV show!

GREAT READING...GREAT SAVINGS...AND A FABULOUS FREE GIFT!

Each book set in Tyler is a self-contained love story; together, the twelve novels stitch the fabric of the community. The covers honor the old American tradition of quilting; each cover depicts a patch of the large Tyler quilt.

With Tyler you can receive a fabulous gift ABSOLUTELY FREE by collecting proofs-of-purchase found in each Tyler book. And use our special Tyler coupons to save on your next TYLER book purchase.

Join your friends at Tyler for the sixth book, SUNSHINE by Pat Warren, available in August.

When Janice Eber becomes a widow, does her husband's friend David provide more than just friendship?

JAYNE ANN KRENTZ

A two-part epic tale from one of today's most popular romance novelists!

Dreams
Parts One & Two

The warrior died at her feet, his blood running out of the cave entrance and mingling with the waterfall. With his last breath he cursed the woman— told her that her spirit would remain chained in the cave forever until a child was created and born there....

So goes the ancient legend of the Chained Lady and the curse that bound her throughout the ages—until destiny brought Diana Prentice and Colby Savager together under the influence of forces beyond their understanding. Suddenly they were both haunted by dreams that linked past and present, while their waking hours were filled with danger. Only when Colby, Diana's modern-day warrior, learned to love, could those dark forces be vanquished. Only then could Diana set the Chained Lady free....

Back by Popular Demand

Janet Dailey
Americana

Janet Dailey takes you on a romantic tour of America through fifty favorite Harlequin Presents novels, each one set in a different state, and researched by Janet and her husband, Bill.

A journey of a lifetime. The perfect collectable series!

August titles   #37 OREGON
To Tell the Truth

#38 PENNSYLVANIA
The Thawing of Mara
